David Trawinski

THE WILLOW'S BEND

DAVID TRAWINSKI

outskirts
press

The Willow's Bend
All Rights Reserved.
Copyright © 2016 David Trawinski
v3.0 r1.0

Cover Image © 2016 Matthew Wisniewski. All rights reserved - used with permission.

Outskirts Press, Inc.
http://www.outskirtspress.com

Soft Cover ISBN: 978-1-4787-7037-4
Hard Cover ISBN: 978-1-4787-7350-4

Outskirts Press and the "OP" logo are trademarks belonging to Outskirts Press, Inc.

PRINTED IN THE UNITED STATES OF AMERICA

Dedicated to the Memory

of

Christopher

Mark

Trawinski

The Willow's Bend

Under the Weight of Shadow's Borne,
Shelter the Assault of Fall's Foreign Wind,
From All Ills That Men Dare Defend.

Nature's Fabric Shred, Not Torn,
Pray I the Penance for All Who've Ever Sinned,
Through This Night I Fear May Never End.

Find Me Safely in the Calm of Morn,
Be I Cast Among the Leaves Much Thinned,
Nestled Safe,
Yet Forever Changed,
Under The Willow's Bend.

Chapter One

Darkness is a weight long borne by the just. It is a weight transferred in the shadows from those who create it, but wish not to bear its heavy mark. It is easily forgotten once transferred, but long and arduously worn by those deceived into accepting it.

STANLEY WISNIEWSKI SAT in the elegant grandeur of the outer office. The dignified tones of the brass-studded, burgundy leather sofa and chairs were magnified by the majesty of the richly burnished mahogany paneling. The angled November sunlight filtered through the three-quartered, wooden- louvered shutters, slicing a seemingly impenetrable fence across the open space between himself and the receptionist. She was matronly, but clearly a lifelong, professional woman, whose first objective was to convince all visitors that she controlled passage into the inner office. She and she alone.

Her reception desk was equally elegant to the rest of the outer office. A Tiffany glass lamp gave her the localized lighting her aging eyes would have desired. Stanley was much aware of the vanities of the aging. He looked down at his own hand, complete with the darkened spots typical of a seventy-year-old man. Perhaps not typical for a man of his age was the fact that both his hands were as steady as rocks. No wasted motion. Not so much as a shake. His eyes were still sharp, although the darkened lighting of the office challenged them. What was the urgency of this meeting? Why here, in his private, Washington DC office?

He used his left hand to rake his somewhat long, gray hair across his forehead in one swift but determined motion, as he slightly cocked his head to the right. He realized he did this so distinctively, with his left palm stretched outward to the watching world. And the world was always watching.

The outer office was visually imposing in its refinement, saying to Stanley, *you are waiting for a very important man*, just as it was designed to do. Marc Constantine was a very important man, seen by many as the man who single-handedly transformed the nation's aerospace and defense industry from a collection of a dozen or so large systems providers, to a handful of dominant industrial giants (with a few also-ran competitors). His vision, and its adroit execution, was responsible for kicking off the series of mergers and acquisitions that reshaped the industry in the 1990s. He was a legend among defense industry leaders, and Stanley had always respected his professionalism and his focus on ethics when they had worked together in the past. Now both were retired for several years. Unlike Marc Constantine's, Stanley's retirement didn't necessitate an opulent office. A career's worth of secrets consume no space, and require no decoration. Stanley looked up in time to catch the gaze of the receptionist.

"Mr. Constantine should not be much longer. Are you sure I can't get you a coffee or hot tea while you wait, Mr. Wisniewski?" Her face was professionally rigid, until after she spoke, when a forced smile cracked across her stoic and indifferent mask. Stanley had noted that she pronounced his name in the Anglicized manner – *wiz-new-ski*.

"No, thank you very much," he responded politely, rising to his feet and standing near her desk. Stanley noticed this unwelcome incursion had her instinctively reaching for her calendar book, fearing Stanley might spy its sacred contents.

"There is one thing, however, which is very small, yet very important to me." he began softly, as if he was speaking in a crowd and wished not to be overheard. "My name, that is. I pronounce my name, *Vish-nev-ski*. It is Polish, and it confuses many people, but I find if I don't correct people, they later fault me for not doing so. I hope you don't mind me bringing this to your attention." He said this in the softest, most gentlemanly tone he could muster, so as not to seem to be scolding her, and to impart an air of a shared secret. Stanley always found this to be effective.

"No, of course not, Mr. *Vish-nev-ski*," she said in a slow strained pronunciation, but correct nonetheless. She forced a second smile that all but betrayed her inner feelings.

Stanley smiled back appreciably. As he returned and sat in the shadows of the dim outer office, he thought of his father. The father that he had already outlived by seventeen years—his father consumed by cancer at the young age of fifty-three.

He was merely keeping one of the three promises he had made to his father on his deathbed each and every time he pronounced his name in the original Polish pronunciation. This was incredibly important to him, and would always be so until he drew his last breath. "*Keep true to your Polish heritage*" was one of his father's three wishes. It had not only stayed a constant vigil in Stanley's life, but was the foundation to the other two.

"*Take care of your mother, the woman is a Saint on Earth*" was the second.

"Protect the weak from the abuses of the strong." To this day he felt he had not fulfilled this third promise. In many ways, he had done just the opposite throughout his life.

Stanley was drifting in the tide of his recollections, his mind floating through a dispersed, co-mingled wash of pride, nostalgia and disappointment.

Suddenly, he was yanked hard from the shadows to the light of the present. The authority that sat before him was ready to perform her most cherished function.

"Mr. *Vish-nev-ski*, Mr. Constantine will see you now," said the receptionist with a practiced, yet beautifully warm smile, as she rose to open the connecting door. Apparently, she had been saving it to add to the grandeur of entering the inner sanctum. She gracefully turned the outer knob and softly pushed open the door.

As he passed her, Stanley could not completely tell if her smile was indeed a practiced part of the act of opening the door, or if she was just pleased with her more confident mastery of pronouncing his last name. He liked to think the latter, but somewhere deep inside, his indecision on the subject gnawed at him. In younger days he would have determined it made no difference. It merely reminded Stanley that his razor sharp senses were finally beginning to wither with the passing of time.

Stanley walked through the door into an even more elegant inner office. As he did, he was surprised to find two men rising from their chairs, not the singular Marc Constantine he was expecting. He recognized the face of the second man instantly, but was having a hard time pulling the name to match. The face was younger, more angular, than that of Constantine's. The body language of the two men did not indicate any deference in any way to each other, other than it was clear that Constantine would initiate the conversation.

They were peers, Stanley thought instantly, but then realized that they weren't true peers, but rather that they had shared a very significant experience. The younger man was the successor to Constantine. He was Everett Roberts, the current CEO of the firm, Global Defense Analytics, that Constantine had so masterfully constructed.

Constantine was showing signs of retirement, although a very active one. He had remained trim for a man of his age, but the paunch around the middle hung softened against his lean frame, and showed nonetheless through the expensive Brooks Brothers suit. While he was three-quarters bald, the male pattern remaining was now a snowy white matte, and not as short-cropped as Stanley remembered.

By contrast, Roberts had a full head of salt and pepper hair, more heavy on salt than pepper. His full coverage was immaculately barbered, and Stanley imagined that it was rarely anything but. His eyes looked sharper than those of Constantine, his movements more efficient, and Stanley was sure his words more direct, though he had not yet spoken.

Everett Roberts awaited patiently the dignity of an introduction.

Suddenly, Stanley became self-aware of his own hair, long and overlapping at his collar. His trimmed beard would be viewed by these men as an indication of the benefit of a relaxed retirement. Stanley drew a half breath and reminded himself that these men had sought him out on urgent business. They were the ones wanting something, possibly desperately. Let them put their problem on the table.

"Stanley, how great to see you again!" Constantine said warmly, not only extending his right hand for a handshake, but grasping Stanley's right elbow in his left hand simultaneously. The move was one taught to executives to show warmth and intimacy for those they had known for some time, or those they wanted to feel so. Stanley remembered this from some of his earliest briefings at the Agency, before he began masquerading in the halls of corporate American defense firms. The training stuck in his mind, because Stanley remembered every niche of society had its own telltale rituals. You either learned them or you were exposed.

"It is very good to see you again, Mr. Constantine," Stanley began. "It has been many years."

"Please, Stanley, call me Marc. No need for formalities among friends." Constantine smiled warmly. Stanley sensed he had slowed, but was still very disarming. "I don't know if you have been introduced to Everett Roberts," Constantine said, turning to the third gentlemen in the room. "Everett is Global Defense Analytics' current CEO. Cleaning up all the problems I left behind, no doubt," he added, chuckling warmly.

"Of course," Stanley said as he shook Roberts' hand and noticed his firm grip. His eyes focused on Stanley's, looking through the surface as if inspecting whether Stanley was worthy of the task at hand. The task was still unknown to Stanley, but the meeting was unexpectedly and speedily called, so Stanley assumed it was quite urgent and quite sensitive.

"It is a pleasure to meet you, Mr. *Vish-nev-ski*." Dead perfect, obviously practiced, but nonetheless very much appreciated. Impressive.

Constantine looked slightly worn and tired compared to Roberts.

His voice was husky with the thickness of the years passed. His solid blue suit, as expensive as it was, hung lifelessly from his frame. His eyes lacked the sparkle Stanley remembered from their last meeting, now some eight years past.

Roberts was an all-together different visual. His tailored, subdued plaid pattern suit fit his trim frame perfectly, his smile and facial countenance exuded warmth, but also a strength of command. Yet he came across as humble, even in the few seconds since they had met. He carried himself with dignity and ceremony. Beneath all this, there was that laser sharp focus one could see in his eyes. Stanley knew Everett Roberts would himself have to retire in a few years due to the firm's bylaws, and somehow Stanley sensed that time would not soften his angles in the same pronounced manner it had with Marc Constantine.

Stanley immediately assessed that Roberts had pressed Constantine into service to assist in solving a very difficult problem. The necessary vanity and ego that Roberts would have had to suppress indicated that this was not a small issue. The use of Constantine's office was indirect, and signaled that this issue was something that demanded discretion.

Marc Constantine continued, "Stanley, we certainly hope your ride down from Baltimore was painless enough. We assume the driver we sent to your home had no trouble finding you. We thought sending Marlow would be the easiest option, as sometimes the DC traffic can be very difficult, even for some of us who have spent much of our careers here, yourself included."

Even for an aged intelligence officer was what he meant. Stanley ignored the hidden reference to his diminished acuity, or their concern about it.

His senses had not betrayed him. Marlow was not a mere driver, but likely sent to size him up on the way.

Stanley responded, "Well, Mr. Marlow was delightful. No problems at all. It was a very nice touch, thank you." I am not very much accustomed to having a driver, Stanley thought, at least not in the U.S. However, in Eastern Europe during my time on station, that was altogether different. The driver was much more than just a driver. Then again, Stanley had already assessed that Mr. Marlow was not a professional driver. He was placed in that role for another reason.

Was he briefing these two men as I waited in the outer office? Was he giving his impressions of whether or not Stanley's eight years of retirement had eroded the skills he honed so sharply at the CIA? Stanley and Marlow's discussions in the car had been brief, but would be telling enough for a professional who knew how to spot the signs of obsolescence.

Constantine turned to Roberts, "Stanley still lives in the home he grew up in in East Baltimore, the Fell's Point neighborhood. Am I right, Stanley? I thought so. Traveled the world throughout his career, but remains living in his childhood home. How often do you hear today of someone not only retiring to their family home, but having lived there all along? I find that so interesting. So refreshing."

"Well, actually, with all my overseas assignments, I feel as if I have hardly lived there at all since I was a boy." Stanley caught himself lowering his head as he said this, and forced himself to make strong eye contact with both men again.

Everett Roberts chimed in, "Certainly a throwback. If I remember correctly, Fells Point is one of the more revitalized areas in Baltimore today. I know my son always gravitates to Fell's Point anytime he and his wife are in Baltimore. They fell in love with the character of the area long ago."

"Well, it is a part of Baltimore that seems to have held on to its charm. It is where I was born, and raised, and where I choose to be. I was formed by the waterfront, and in many ways, it forms me still."

Stanley thought of the nightlife in the neighborhood. The crowds that washed over the area now like an angry tide most every weekend night. They came for the allure of the uneven, cobblestone streets, and row-house bars that angled distinctively away from the street front. The trendy loft homes converted from warehouses. This now defined the area that Stanley remembered so differently as he grew up as a boy exploring this working harbor front. Time transforms everything, Stanley thought, everything and everyone.

Roberts broke the silence. "I am always amazed at the overall revital-ization of that area. Tremendous foresight by the city planners. Your home is very nicely located, indeed."

Recognizing the last comment was meant to cap off that segment of the conversation, Stanley decided to extend it nonetheless. It was important to him.

"Yes. I would agree. More important to me is that it is the home my father and mother lived in when they first came to this country from Poland after World War II. As far as the revitalization, we all get lucky sometimes. Twenty-five years ago it seemed to be heading in the other direction entirely." Stanley now sensed the preliminaries were now over.

"Stanley, please have a seat," Constantine said, guiding him over to the executive conference table, rather than sitting at the desk itself.

The three men sat at the table, and Constantine began in a very serious voice, as if necessitated by the significance of their three reflections floating detached in the highly lustered and burnished mahogany tabletop.

"Stanley, I recommended you to Everett to help us investigate a very delicate matter. My recommendation was based on our experience together in 1985 on the Project INDIGO case. I was very impressed with your abilities then and since. And while we know you are retired now, we need to turn to someone we can trust for a very speedy yet insightful investigation. I'll let Everett fill you in on the facts."

Stanley's heart sank with the mention of Project INDIGO. While it was successful for Constantine and his firm, it was a dark spot in Stanley's own recollection of his career. He met every objective the agency and Constantine's firm had set, but in the end failed himself. More importantly, he reminded himself that he failed his father's third request, *"Protect the weak from the abuses of the strong."*

It was the memory he could not bear to revisit, yet it was the reason Constantine was requesting his assistance today. He could not bear to think of Bryce Weldon, God rest his soul. Bryce Weldon was the young engineer entrapped in a traitor's plot. Stanley had successfully handed him to the agency, and it was the agency that ended up destroying him. It reminded Stanley of the abuses his own father suffered at the hands of the powerful early in his life. It reminded Stanley of the purity of the life his father lived, with what was left of the broken shell of his existence. Bryce Weldon was denied even an existence.

"Mr. Wisniewski," Roberts began, "three nights ago, on Saturday night, our firm lost a dear member of our leadership team. I don't know if you are aware of this as of yet, but Mr. Ted Barber, who headed our International Office in London, was found drowned in the canals of Amsterdam. Our research to date reveals that Mr. Barber, recently divorced, was having a liaison with a young lady, also an overseas employee of ours. She was also found dead nearby in Mr. Barber's hotel room. A very strange case, and due to Dutch privacy laws, there is very little information available to us as his employer, at least at this early point of the investigation."

Clearly, this matter was very sensitive to both men, but Stanley sensed they had not gotten to the real issue yet. He could read the look in Roberts' worried eyes. It was time to draw out more information.

"If I may," Stanley began, "it seems to me you wouldn't need a retired intelligence officer to research this. In fact, I really wouldn't have access to all the sources I would need. There may not be much I can do here."

"Yes. Yes, of course," Roberts continued. "We don't expect you to research Mr. Barber's death itself. We have a security team working on that with the Dutch authorities, and, of course, the families involved. We will give you access to their findings, as appropriate. But this event touches another event that is imminent in our corporation's future. In nine days, at our next Board of Directors Meeting, we are to name the appointee to replace our Chief Operating Officer, who will be announcing his retirement."

Roberts continued, "As this is the number two position in the corporation, it must be approved by our Board. One of the candidates, in fact the leading candidate, is Langston Powell, head of our Aerospace Operating Unit. This appointment will effectively be my successor when I decide, in due time, to retire. Incidentally, Mr. Powell had dinner with Mr. Barber in Amsterdam on the evening that he passed away. So clearly...," Robert's voice trailed off, giving

Stanley an opportunity to demonstrate he understood the subtleties of the request that was being made.

"So clearly, the firm needs to assure that Mr. Powell is in no way connected to Mr. Barber's death," Stanley interceded. "And since there is little factual data to base this upon, you are looking for my insights after reviewing the case, and perhaps after interviewing Mr. Powell."

"Precisely, but perhaps not so directly," Marc Constantine responded. "Mr. Powell is aware he is under consideration for the COO position, and our inquiries need to be done in a very non-intrusive manner. This inquiry action we are asking you to undertake is being sanctioned by the Board of Directors, but will be disavowed if this investigation becomes known to the financial world. It absolutely must be concluded by the Board of Directors meeting in nine days' time."

"That explains the reason for having this meeting in Mr. Constantine's retirement office," Stanley said. "It's not an office of the firm itself, so it keeps things a little cleaner should I decide not to accept this assignment."

"I was told you were quick and insightful, Mr. Wisniewski, and so I see." Roberts again picked up the conversation. "I have no need to flatter you, but I do have need of your skills. I am told you have an uncanny ability to read people."

Roberts said this in a tone to suggest that Stanley could perhaps read him now. "I am very nervous about selecting you for this assignment, but I am deferring to the judgment of Marc Constantine in this matter. The ticking of the clock is all that keeps me from researching your selection yet further."

"Your ability to see the subtleties in this, assess the intangibles, and frankly determine the innocence of Mr. Powell," continued Roberts, "is what is of most value to us. Should your report come back without that conviction, we are prepared to move to our second choice, clearly a lesser candidate. We all believe very strongly in Mr. Powell's innocence."

Or wished they could, Stanley thought. These men know the nature of the beast better than any, and they have their concerns.

"Why not defer the decision? Name Powell as the replacement at a future meeting of the board?" Stanley watched the faces of the two men intently.

"An obvious question," Roberts responded. "I am afraid it is too late for that, as Wall Street has already been alerted to our need to replace our COO. He is very ill, and for some reason felt it necessary to hide this from us for some time. Although he desires to continue in his capacity, his weakening frame is no longer up to the demands of the position. We have assisted him in seeing this, and we fear he has, at best, several weeks left with the firm. His replacement needs to be named now."

Stanley quipped, "It is ironic, I think, that the same privacy laws that led to his dire need to be replaced, are in fact now interfering with your clearing his successor."

"Ironic indeed," said Roberts. "However, it creates a windfall opportunity for yourself."

"Stanley," offered the older, heavier voice of Constantine, "here are the terms. We believe them to be very generous. $350K to be paid through my office. Half up front. Half on completion of the task. We are prepared to wire the initial payment to your bank this morning."

He slid a leather portfolio across the table to Stanley, documenting the deal. Stanley reviewed the same numbers on the single sheet inside. Very generous indeed, only magnifying the importance this matter held to these men. This spoke volumes to Stanley, specifically of their concerns that the Saturday night dinner in Amsterdam was more than just a coincidence on Langston Powell's part. And Ted Barber lay dead in an Amsterdam morgue.

Stanley looked intently at the sheet. He drew his thumb and forefinger across his trimmed gray beard, to give the illusion he was anticipating passing on the request.

"If I do it, I will need access to your firm's most sensitive data on both Mr. Powell and Mr. Barber. Data that certainly will violate your own company's privacy policies," Stanley stated, not waiting for a response. "I will also need fifty thousand dollars in operational funds. I cannot assure you that I will need this full amount, but for the sake of my accepting this assignment, please assume it will be consumed fully."

"Stanley, that seems a little excessive," began Constantine, "we will certainly reimburse any expenses that you may incur, but..."

Roberts interceded forcibly. "Thank you, Marc, but that won't be a problem at all. Stanley needs these funds, I am sure, for some delicate information gathering. Not something that we can exactly expect a receipt for. Stanley, we will have it deposited to your account this morning as well. We will also provide any and all information that you require."

"Then I agree to conduct this investigation for you."

Stanley's commitment was simply stated, with no ambiguity.

Roberts looked forcibly into Stanley's eyes, as if he were a man being forced into an action he knew he might regret having hastily taken.

"Can you leave tomorrow morning?" he asked.

"For Amsterdam?" queried Stanley.

"No, for California," answered Roberts. "That's where you will find Langston Powell."

Chapter Two

THE DRIVER'S NAME was Marlow. It was unclear if this was his real name, or the name he was using for this operation. Stanley did not care which was true. Constantine and Roberts informed Stanley that Marlow would be the contact for Stanley to pass his requests through. Clearly, he was the cut-out. An expendable link, someone who they trusted, but who could also be counted on to take the fall for whatever problems arose from this "investigation". More clearly, he was not a professional driver, as Stanley readily observed in the DC midday traffic.

As Marlow negotiated his exit from the District, joined the heavy flow of traffic up I-95, and dropped into downtown Baltimore on his way to Fell's Point, Stanley thought how unusual this situation really was. A corporation so dependent on the financial and defense communities' confidence in its leadership team's strength now had to make a snap call on Langston Powell, given the Barber affair. Why were they even concerned? Did Langston Powell have a history that called his character into question? What was he even doing in Amsterdam on a Saturday night?

The Lincoln Town Car soon rattled along the cobblestone streets of Fell's Point. Its ride smoothed as it turned cautiously onto the asphalt-paved but narrow Shakespeare Street. It was early fall, and the feeling of intimacy was enhanced by the crimson-hued trees desperately clinging to their bloom of turning, dying leaves. Everyone knew these would fall away in the coming days, leaving only the nakedness of the limbs to endure the coming winter.

The town car negotiated the street with its parked vehicles on both sides, until it came to 1633 Shakespeare. The form-stoned front of the house, a stuccoed imitation stone, so beloved in old Baltimore, was adorned with an original stained glass transom, both holdovers from an earlier time. The rest of the houses on the block were grit blasted red brick fronts, the form-stone long removed in an attempt to comply with the trendy chic of the current era.

Stanley had always likened it to the vanities of the earlier generations being stripped away by the vanities of their offspring, and he chose not to participate.

No other house on this tree-lined block had kept its stained glass, numbered transom, or traditional form-stone edifice. As far as Stanley was concerned, the others had traded their character for the convenience of a quick profitable resale of their grit blasted facade. Stanley alone had opted for the past.

Stanley perceived Marlow noting all this during the morning pickup. If only my hand-painted "old world" storm door window screens had not been lost to vandals some ten years earlier. That surely would have peaked Mr. Marlow's interest.

Marlow delivered Stanley at his row home door, pausing only to bring in the briefcase containing the relevant files that had been pre-selected for Stanley's overnight review. Clearly Stanley's acceptance had been anticipated.

The briefcase was handed to Stanley in his living room, the door open, the idling car clogging the funnel that was Shakespeare Street. Leaves of brilliant red and brown hues swirled in the afternoon sunshine around the car. The briefcase, its weight passing palpably from Marlow to Stanley, cemented the relationship between them—all of them. Stanley felt the gravity of this transfer.

"I'll pick you up at six AM for the drive to the airport. If you need anything at all just call me on the phone that is in the briefcase. The instructions are quite easy to follow. Don't destroy any of the files in the briefcase–they are numbered and watermarked. We will need to get those back when you are finished with them. The operational funds you requested, as well as your initial payment, have already been electronically transferred to the account number you provided Mr. Constantine. This has been confirmed."

That was quick, Stanley thought. He stared at, but said nothing to Marlow.

"Thought you might want to get a jump on things. The funds transferred as we were driving up I-95. I got a text confirming that." Marlow's face seemed to indicate he was anxious to get back to the Town Car before someone got the idea to slip into the idling beast.

Stanley smiled. The text no doubt came in on a burner–a cell phone that was disposable and not traceable to the firm. If only he knew the agency would have no trouble identifying the call by the trace of the cell phone pings from Constantine's office to Shakespeare Street, thus tying it to Marlow.

"One last thing, Mr. *Vish-nev-ski*. I will be your operational handler for this effort. All contact will be to me, and not to Mr. Constantine or Mr. Roberts. As far as you are concerned, today's meeting did not take place. I am the handler to whom all your needs and desires should be addressed."

Stanley raised his eyes to look intently into Marlow's. The man spoke like a professional, someone from Stanley's stock and trade.

"I suppose you will be my confessor also," Stanley stated sarcastically.

"If you need a confessor, my friend, you are in the wrong trade," Marlow said with a half-smile. "I will pick you up here at 0600 tomorrow to take you to the airport. Everything is arranged, just bring enough clothes for a week, business attire. I assume you have..."

"Don't worry, I think I can pull it off," said Stanley, smiling back at his driver.

Marlow climbed back into the idling town car and drove carefully down the length of Shakespeare Street, focusing on his mirrors to make sure that they cleared the narrow, leafy, fall lane formed by the parked cars on either side. None belonged to Stanley, having given up that vanity a few years earlier. Stanley no longer had the need to drive. Marlow turned onto the much wider Bond Street and was gone.

And so Stanley had the sensation of being in a skiff, pushing off for a long journey upriver. Provisioned, but not really knowing what lie ahead. Given the boredom of his long retirement, this excited him.

The afternoon passed into deep shadows. After locking up 1633 Shakespeare Street, Stanley took his ritual walk along Fell's Point's cobblestoned streets. Today it helped him focus his thoughts on all that would have to be done before his departure in the morning.

He walked, following the cobblestones from Broadway up to Thames Street, past Brown's Wharf and its modern loft warehouse homes above the storefronts. Stagnant, worn and dying just a generation ago, Fell's Point was revitalized in the present.

Bookstores, brass works, second-hand music shops and art galleries were interspersed with bars that drew in nightlife. The overall effect was much like the seedy entertainment district of a college town. Minus the rigors and tensions of higher learning.

Then Stanley was walking briskly past the Recreation Pier he had played on as a boy, still dressed in the false Baltimore Police Station livery long left over by the national television show filmed there years ago. Its aged and decaying front played true to the pier itself, the only element of Fell's Point that paid tribute to the hard-working history of this area. The tugboats along its side bobbed in the rough harbor waters like silent sentinels to the past.

He continued his ritual by marching up the angle formed by Fell's Street to Henderson's Wharf, with its own versions of lofts for the modern urban lifestyle. He proceeded along the parking pier, taking in the sights of the choppy, blue-gray harbor under the early November overcast sky. The wind tossed thick ropes of white foam across the water's undulating surface. Stanley breathed in the salted taste of the harbor. Stanley then circled back to where the pier joined Fells Street, before righting onto Wolfe Street, down to Lancaster Street, and then back to Broadway.

The foot of Broadway was the observed landing site of the founders of the city. It was once the primary sailing port, as evidenced by the cobblestones themselves. These were the very stones used as ballast from the ships coming to port from England, and beyond. Only fitting that they still leave their mark on this city. History has a way of leaving its marks, healed badly like old scars.

As Stanley turned back onto Shakespeare Street, he was reminded of the insensitivity of modernity as Broadway's cobblestones gave way to its congealed asphalt roadway. The cobblestones would have completed the scene of the tree-lined row homes on either side. The tall green, metallic street lamps, original to his boyhood memories, began flickering their silos of warmth for the cold night to come.

Stanley walked to the street's end at Bond Street before doubling back to his narrow doorway. Some habits die hard. Stanley found himself back at his entryway just as the afternoon was dissolving into dusk. He slid in the front door, locking it as he entered, knowing he was in for the evening.

He checked that the briefcase was still untouched on his kitchen table where he left it. It was. He fixed himself a light dinner and took to packing immediately afterward. Best to complete that while he still had the energy.

After packing, he took his Heckler & Koch nine millimeter pistol from its place in the side table closest to the kitchen. This he did every night, one of the necessities of living in the city. To the casual eye, he was but an old man living alone on a secluded side street, and that could be tempting as the city night fell.

An hour later, Stanley found himself at his small kitchen table. It was a carved oak table with a hand-painted metal surface from the 1940s. It was one of the first possessions of his mother and father when they arrived to this town, indeed to this house, immediately after World War II. The hand-painted surface was an elegant pattern with swans alighting on a placid pond in front of a country cottage in the four corners, connected by an intricate border. The serenity of this scene would have appealed to these immigrants whose life had been anything but serene up until that point.

With the contents of the briefcase spread before him like a deck of cards fanned out in front of a gambler, he began to review the arrangement of files. His mind began to drift. The memories of the row home began to call to him. Stanley decided not to indulge himself. He stayed on task.

Stanley reached his hand across the table, smoothly wrapping it around the ice cold bottle of Belvedere Vodka he had just taken from his freezer. He looked at the palace on the label, remembering his many times standing outside of its elegant facade in Warsaw. He poured the vodka into one of the cut crystal tumblers he had hand carried back from Warsaw for his mother. Long gone, he remembered her and the tortured life she endured. His eyes moistened, before he drank hard and fought back the ghosts of the departed.

They obeyed for just a bit.

He allowed himself only one drink per evening, and most nights didn't bother at all. Tonight demanded his ritual be played out fully. His favorite collection of Chopin nocturnes played in the background. Stanley was at peace with himself, isolated from the world outside his door.

Stanley loved the music of Frederic Chopin. Especially the nocturnes, which like most of the valued recollections of life, have to be felt deep in one's core, as does faith itself. Chopin, his life itself so contemptuously scarred, was the author of the Polish soul. One could not be Polish, even in this case Polish-American, and not be moved by the poetry of Chopin's works. The nocturnes' softened sadness were the spirit that nestled in the house. They were the Polish soul.

Stanley took from its place the portable disc player he had kept since the late eighties. He had taken this device all over the world, along with his collection of the works of Chopin as interpreted by Arthur Rubinstein. This he would need for the ensuing trip. Stanley had shunned the entire digital revolution, except for a single laptop that he used very irregularly to communicate with the outside world. It was a holdover from his operational days.

As the warmth of the vodka ripped across Stanley's state of grace, the mournful elegance of Chopin's nocturnes carried him back to a simpler childhood. It was a peaceful, but delicate illusion, soon to be ruptured as a young adult by the ever-present remains of the war, carried forever as scars, both literally and figuratively, by his father.

He remembered, nearly forty years earlier, sitting on the bed of his dying father. The same bedroom that was above his very head on the second floor of the row home in which he now sat. The year was 1975. He was a young man of just 30, having recently completed his graduate degree from Loyola of Maryland. His degree was in economics, but his love was languages—Polish, Russian, German and French.

His love of language was passed to him by his father. Many of his earliest recollections were of his father teaching him the subtleties of dialects. He soaked up languages quickly and effortlessly. The Polish spoken in the home was his foundation, later expanded by the necessity of English for the world beyond his front door, although many in his neighborhood spoke excellent, fluent Polish as well. Next, through the teachings of his father, he learned German and Russian, if not fluently, certainly conversationally.

French came later due to the full scholarship provided to him by a local politician, who lived in the neighborhood herself. This could never happen today, with the ever-dangling ax of fiscal conservancy, but had it not then, Stanley's life would have changed dramatically.

There would have been no career with the agency, no Bryce Weldon and no Project INDIGO, no network in Eastern Europe, and certainly no Ted Barber/Langston Powell affair, with which he entertained his talents tonight.

Stanley had started his career after having been recruited by the agency based on his proficiency in languages. He had just returned from his introductory posting in Europe–his field trials, so to speak.

The Chopin echoed mournfully yet poetically throughout the modest kitchen–just a nook really. Stanley reviewed the files between pulls of vodka. He noticed the files–all paper, none electronic–were individually numbered and watermarked so that they could be traced.

Corporations were paranoid when it came to leaking executive appointments, but given the potentially scandalous nature of Ted Barber's demise, they were deathly afraid of electronic hacking and a viral internet file with which to contend.

Stanley now had to contend with the ghosts of his memories, which had returned.

"Stanislaus, come close, my Stashew," Stanley could hear his father's voice in his memory. "Come, my boy, sit your *dupa* here on my bed. I need to talk to you tonight. Tonight you are mine."

The voice was nothing more than a heavy whisper. His always frail frame by then was nearly consumed by the cancer he was fighting a losing battle against. He lay flat, his already dead eyes focused on the cracked plaster ceiling, only stealing glances of the young man sitting beside him, as if full eye contact was too painful to bear.

"My Stashew, you know I am dying?" he asked plaintively in his native language.

"Yes, Father. I know this. This is why I came home from Europe now," the young Stanley replied in his fluent Polish.

"My Stashew, you do not know but I am already dead. I have been dead for many years, only you have kept a wisp of breath in my soul. You are the reason I am here to this day," his father said slowly while tears began to pool in the lifeless stones that were once eyes.

Stanley knew what was to come, or so he thought. He could still smell the muster of the plastered walls, the peeling cracked dried out wallpaper, and the general smell of decay that permeated the darkened room. Smells and memories that drove Stanley to renovate the small home, had somehow survived the renovation. The bedroom itself Stanley left intact, the only interior room saved from the renovator.

In his memory, his father strenuously labored to finish the remainder of this conversation in his best Russian. Stanley knew this was to keep his mother from overhearing, despite her being downstairs.

"My boy," he struggled, "you must make me three promises. I must hear them from your very lips." He was forcing his sullen watered eyes to find Stanley's tear-filled own.

"Relax, Father, I am here," Stanley said, grasping his father's frail skeletal hand. "I am going nowhere," he replied in Russian.

"My boy, promise me this..." The old man was rushing to get whatever it was out. He had to get it out before there was no time left.

"Promise me, three simple things."

"Yes, Father, what are these promises?"

His father continued, tears running down his gaunt cheeks. "Promise me first that you will take care of your mother until our Lord calls her home. She is a saint among women, and she will need you."

"Yes, of course, Father, I will care for Mother always, I swear," the young Stanley replied.

"I ask for promises, not oaths. Promise like a man. Do not swear. Do not be coarse. Be the man I raised you to be..." The labor of his breathing indicated his disappointment with young Stanley.

"Yes, of course, I promise. I am sorry for my poor choice of words."

The father rested, gathering strength for the next promise. "Promise me you will always respect and indulge your Polish culture. This is very dear to me, my boy. Promise me no matter what you learn in life, no matter what, you will remain Polish. Always be proud to be Polish."

This was a familiar discussion that Stanley and his father had had over many years. Do not Americanize, do not forgo your Polish language, your culture, your upbringing. "Yes, father, this I promise also."

His father's hand grasped young Stanley's forearm, indicating the third promise was the most important yet.

"Stashew, I know you grow strong. I hear it in your voice. I know what you do, I know your work, and what they send you to Europe for."

He rested to attempt to catch his breath. Stanley knew his father did not really know the nature of his assignments. Stanley had labored to keep this from his father, as another burden he needed not to bear.

"Stashew, promise me fully you will never take advantage of the weak. No matter how strong you become, defend the weak. Show compassion; be human. It is the abuses of the strong that are rained upon the backs of the weak, the poor."

"Yes, Father, I promise this and all three promises. I will live my life as you have asked, I can only hope to live as good a life as you."

These words seemed to beat the breath out of his father. His head fell back; his eyes returned to the ceiling. The tears now trailed back down the sides of his head, finding the hollows of his ears.

"I have not lived a life," he concluded. "I am here but to bear the marks of the beast."

Stanley watched as his father, with a slow, strained motion, exposed his greatest secret, pulling his sleeve to shamelessly reveal the tattooed numbers of Auschwitz. It was a secret Stanley knew too well, despite his father hiding it from him. But his father had never willingly exposed it to him before.

Stanley touched the indigo numeric markings on his wrist. His father had never had them removed, nor had his father had ever defaced them himself in any way. Stanley knew he would not talk of this time, as it was too painful a burden to bear. But was it a burden he needed to shed before dying? Stanley sensed so.

"These are the marks of the beast. Many think the beast is dead, but the beast lives in the darkness of men's hearts, waiting to return. This is why I ask of you these three promises. I have much more to tell you, but I am too tired at this moment. Allow an old man to rest."

The old man was fifty-three. He had lived an intolerable life. It was not a life but a survival. More of a test of a man, stripped of his own spirit long ago, fearing now the price he must soon pay for the rage of his youth, against the darkness unleashed by the beast.

Through the years, the tears reached Stanley as he finished his vodka. The Chopin had long ceased playing. Stanley sobbed quietly to himself.

Chapter Three

MARLOW ARRIVED PROMPTLY at six AM to take Stanley to the plane. Stanley was ready, sharply focused after a soundly refreshing sleep. This after getting an internet message, encoded and encrypted, off to his former companion Jean Paul in Paris to get him moving toward Amsterdam, where he would inquire into the details of the Barber drowning.

Marlow was on time, arriving in a simple blue suit, white shirt accompanied by a red and white striped regent's tie. After helping Stanley with his bags, they headed east along Aliceanna and then Boston Streets, so Stanley assumed he was heading to the Harbor Tunnel Thruway to the Baltimore Washington Thurgood Marshall International Airport. Why they had ever changed the name from Friendship Airport, Stanley couldn't understand – it was simple, welcoming and easy to remember. The things that are forsaken for the sake of progress.

When Marlow drove past the entrance ramps to both the Harbor Tunnel Thruway and the Francis Scott Key Tunnel, Stanley asked Marlow where he was taking him.

"I'm sorry, sir, I should have been more specific," Marlow began. "You won't be flying commercial this morning. I've been instructed to take you to the company jet. We are heading out to Martin State Airport where the fleet is based. I believe they have you lined up on the Gulfstream."

"Incredible" was Stanley's only reply.

So Marlow pulled directly onto the tarmac at the small regional airport that at one time was part of the World War II-era defense plant just across the road. These plants produced the magnificent B-26 Marauder aircraft that helped turn the tide of World War II. Stanley could not help but notice the A-10 aircraft that neatly lined up across the tarmac, waiting to be sortied by the Air National Guard.

Stanley always loved these tank-busting Warthogs, with their remarkable low altitude handling, complemented by the toughness of their titanium cockpit enclosures and the lethality of their depleted uranium rounds. It was a combination of agility, strength and deadliness Stanley respected, or even envied. Like Stanley himself, they seemed not to fit into the needs of today.

Climbing aboard the jet, Stanley found himself facing a cabin that could readily seat eleven passengers – four along a small table, two seats facing each other just across a small aisle, another pair of facing seats just behind those, and across the aisle and behind the table seating, a small sofa lined the fuselage interior, which was capable of holding a final three passengers. The interior was businesslike in motifs of tan and light blues.

Stanley began to sit in the most forward-facing seat across the aisle from the table.

"Good morning, Mr. *Vis-nev-ski* (again, dead perfect pronunciation), would you mind being seated at the table?" The voice was

young and courteous.

Stanley turned to respond to see a man in his thirties in a white jacket.

Marlow, carrying aboard Stanley's briefcase after having his other bag loaded in the aft luggage area, made the introduction.

"Stanley," he began. "This is Curtis. He'll be seeing after us on the flight this morning."

"Why take me on the company plane when you have gone to great lengths to keep my connection clear of Global Defense Analytics?" Stanley replied quixotically.

"Technically, only I am on the manifest, Stanley," answered Marlow with a heavy smile and a very subtle wink. "Nonetheless, you will benefit from the hours saved by not traveling commercial, and I thought I could take advantage of the flight time to review the briefing materials with you."

They both strapped in, facing each other across the table, and soon were taxiing across the tarmac to the runway. Stanley looked out his window to see Marlow's car still where it had been stopped next to the jet.

"The ground crew will take care of that, don't worry. Everything here is all about wheels up," Marlow laughed.

Indeed, it had been no more than three minutes after they arrived before they were barreling down the runway. Certainly, the way to travel. They were no sooner clear of the runway and climbing out before Curtis brought them both hot coffee and fruit and ham breakfast plates. He soon disappeared forward not to be seen again until mid-flight, and after that just before touchdown.

Stanley stared out the window as they traversed the bay. He recognized the dual spans of the Chesapeake Bay bridges. In a few seconds they were over Annapolis and turning westward. As they picked at their breakfasts, Marlow started on his discourse.

"So, as you may have seen last night, Powell and Barber had an interconnected past." He stated openly.

So, Stanley thought, a nice friendly chat to see how much of the file materials Stanley had absorbed. "Someone is concerned I am past my prime?" he thought.

Stanley used his left hand, palm open and outward, to rake his gray mane of hair up off his forehead. What had once been an operational tell had now become habit. He knew this could be deadly were he still active. Now it was just the indulgence of an old man's habit.

He took a drink of his coffee and responded.

"Ted Barber was the up and coming executive. Brilliant engineer–a systems engineer, if I am correct. He worked his way up the ladder on various platforms, that is aircraft, before he made his mark on the Daedalus Destroyer Drone program."

Stanley pointed to a picture of the stealthy high altitude drone he referred to. Stanley knew it as the deadly accurate killer the Agency had deployed throughout the Middle East in the GWOT–the Global War on Terror.

"Barber's primary claim to fame was his ability to fix the early versions of the aircraft's integrated software. The drone's software was crashing so much that they actually had to put a reset button on the remote flight control panel. The early versions of the Daedalus

Destroyer were sold to the Air Force. At least one crashed due to the software issues. Barber was assigned to it. He led a team of twenty that stabilized the drone's software in six months."

Stanley continued his summary of the reading from the night before.

"This was a major accomplishment that ultimately got him the VP and Chief Engineer position in the program–the highest technical authority for the world's most complex drone program. Not bad for someone not quite yet 45- years-old. As I recall that is where Langston Powell entered the picture."

Stanley continued before Marlow could interrupt. "Powell was a corporate climber, but from the Missiles Division. He was about fifty. This was his first foray into the highly parochial Aerospace Division. He was selected as the overall program manager of their most complex drone program—the Daedalus Destroyer. A real dark horse selection, but the corporation was intentionally trying to cross-pollinate its leadership between its four operating units–Aerospace, Missiles and Air Defense, Space, and Network Solution Systems. Besides, these drones were already formidably deadly because they were integrated with the missiles that Powell had previously worked on as program manager."

Marlow was impressed with the level of detail that Stanley had absorbed from the files overnight.

Stanley continued. "Langston Powell would soon convince the CIA that the Daedalus Destroyer could be even more deadly by integrating electronic collection sensors onto its already stealthy airframe. It became the deadly sentinel of Afghanistan, Iraq and Yemen over the last ten years. It paid for itself by freeing up U-2 overflights and saved satellite passes for only the highest prioritized targets – priority made by the information from the Daedalus Destroyer Drone collections."

"Exactly correct." Marlow interrupted. "But I don't recall that last bit being in the dossier."

"It wasn't," said Stanley. His turn to smile wryly.

Stanley continued. "Barber and Powell were pretty tight over the next two years. Powell was using him to gain favor with the executive leadership by mentoring him, advancing his career through prestigious training assignments as well as backing him for the highest level of corporate awards. Powell culminated this process by promoting Barber to be his deputy program manager."

Stanley took a breath and continued, "Everything was going as well as it could. The drones were cranking out 30 platforms a year, a major cash cow for the firm, and with a really nice profit margin thanks to the secret CIA budgets. It was performing exceptionally well. Together, Powell and Barber had gotten the Daedalus program through Initial Operational Capability."

Stanley knew that IOC was the major event that allowed it to be formally ready for the inventory of the United States. Ready for War. Marlow could see he was familiar with the process.

Stanley pressed on. "Despite this not having occurred yet, the drones had already been secretly rushed into service in Afghanistan and Yemen. Barber was well on his way as the next generation of senior executive, and Powell was well positioned to move up to his current assignment heading the entire Aerospace Division."

"Then the wheels came off, at least for Barber. Powell was promoted to head Aerospace. But Barber was passed over for the Daedalus Destroyer program manager selection. Shortly afterward, Barber quietly had himself a nasty little divorce. Seems his wife was totally tired of raising their three young children while Barber was chasing his career—and other things—six days a week in the office."

The other things he chased included skirts, based on where the story was headed, but Stanley knew Marlow had understood the inference.

What Marlow understood was that he would have to wedge his way back into the conversation. "Again, I see you were reading pretty heavily between the lines. Very perceptive and dead right, spot on."

Stanley mentally marked the last two words. So very corporate. He was now convinced that Marlow was a trusted executive in the stable of Everett Roberts. A direct but deniable contact who was on the flight manifest, while Stanley wasn't. Very convenient. Very plausibly deniable.

Earlier he had begun to wonder if Marlow was from outside the firm, or worse, an implant of the Board of Directors. Or an agent of Langston Powell himself.

The jet was smooth through the flight to this point, but now was shaking off the effects of some modest turbulence.

"This jet is so small compared to a commercial passenger jet, how can it be as safe?" he asked Marlow. He could feel a slight fishtailing of the cabin. Stanley had been on agency jets this size, but rarely, throughout his career. Certainly, he'd never been on one to transport himself alone.

"Stanley, it's all about the thrust to weight ratio," Marlow explained.

A wry smile creased his clean corporate facade. You might be a cloak and dagger spook with a windfall assignment, but you better get used to the corporate *accoutrements*, or you will be soon found out, he thought.

Marlow continued out loud, "This jet's got so much more control because its thrust to weight ratio cannot be touched by a commercial jet. It is also able to fly higher generally than commercial aviation jets. I suspect we are at about 41,000 feet right now, above almost all the commercial flights. This allows the pilots to fly more direct flight plans, shaving significant flight time. You've already seen how fast we can board, disembarking is even faster."

Stanley listened intently, hoping the mild turbulence would soon end. It did, and the remainder of the flight was exceptionally smooth.

Curtis came from the cockpit to refresh the coffees and tend to the official and unofficial passengers. He quickly disappeared forward again. Stanley assumed this was pre-arranged with Marlow.

Stanley picked up the trail of the conversation again. "I do have a simple question for you, Mr. Marlow. If Barber was dealing with his divorce, and wasn't considered a candidate to replace Powell as the drone program lead, why was he put up as a candidate to head the London office?"

"Just Marlow, not Mr. Marlow" was the initial response.

"Is that Marlow as a first name or last?" asked Stanley.

"Just Marlow" came the response. Stanley dropped it.

Marlow was eager to add something to the conversation. "London office. Right. It was simple, Powell was backing him a hundred percent. And since Aerospace dominated the work in the UK, Powell carried the day."

Continuing, Marlow explained, "Ted Barber was well equipped for the position from a resume standpoint, and quickly picked up the international aspect of the job. London's not a bad place for a newly made bachelor to take up residence. Lots of side trips to the continent in the two years he was in the position. Paris, Vienna, Venice, and several trips to Amsterdam. All on his own nickel mind you. We were quick to check that out."

"How many trips to Amsterdam?"

Marlow was quick to respond. "Six by our count. We checked that too. Pretty evenly spaced."

Stanley arched his eyebrows. "Any evidence of a drug problem?"

"We looked for that. No evidence whatsoever. Clean as a whistle in that regard."

Stanley wondered why he would go to Amsterdam if not the fringe benefits. What if Barber were dealing secrets to the competition? After all, as chief engineer on the Daedalus Destroyer he would have been knowledgeable of vital information on Stealth, Maneuverability and Operational data. Amsterdam would be a convenient site for trading that, but likely the other side would want to rotate locations for their own security. This Stanley could find out pretty quickly.

Stanley had been considering accessing information from Marlow. He decided to make the demand in a very direct manner. He felt comfortable with Marlow. Stanley thought he could work with him.

"I would like to get some files from you. I need both Powell and

Barber's files on lawsuits, ethics cases, and Special Access Required programs. I'd like to have this by tomorrow night, if I am to meet the nine-day deadline."

Marlow winced. "The ethics files may be difficult, but I was told to give you whatever you asked for. I'll work on it right away. I'll call it in and should have a response when I get back to DC this afternoon."

"So you aren't joining me in Palmdale?" Stanley asked.

"No, I am merely here for the conversation." Marlow smiled broadly. "The manifest will show I was in Palmdale for only a brief but very important review. Not much more than the time it takes to refuel and re-provision the aircraft."

After a little more general discussion on Barber and Powell, Marlow switched topics.

"Let's go over your cover for this trip. Powell knows we are flying you in, thinking you are Howard Burnett's, the firm's CFO, outside specialist on Financial Risk Management. In your briefcase are business cards, with a complimentary, but fictitious, fully-functioning answering service. You will be joining up with the INAR team, excuse me, the Independent Non Advocacy Review Team – I am so used to these damn acronyms I forget myself. The INAR started Monday reviewing the latest CIA drone program proposal being readied for submitting to the government. Should be a perfect cover."

Defense firms typically would bring in independent teams of experts to review proposals, or sometimes do failure investigations of products in the field. Non-advocate just meant they were usually not on the immediate program under review, but from within the firm elsewhere. Only occasionally was a total outsider brought in–especially in the financial reviews. Stanley thought this could be tricky to pull off undetected.

"You'll be expected to ask questions relative to the risk of the proposal," Marlow said.

"Shouldn't be too tough. My being quiet more often than not will be perceived as playing my cards close."

"You have a feel for the rest of the INAR team members?" asked Marlow.

"Yes, I saw the business cards and list of the INAR team members. Is Burnett let in on this exercise?" Stanley asked.

"Sure, he is. There are four of us: Burnett, Constantine, Roberts, and myself. The Board only knows we are doing background on Powell and other candidates."

"What exactly is your role in all this?" Stanley had decided to catch him off-guard with the unexpectedly direct question. Marlow gave him a silent but icy stare, as if to say, don't ask me that again.

Marlow's face then cracked with a warmth he seemed strained to muster up.

"Me? I am only the errand boy. No more than a clerk, really. The others, especially Mr. Roberts, are the ones you are working for." Marlow thought, if he plays me again, I will totally shut down the conversation.

Stanley scanned his face, looking for a tell-tale twitch, or nervous hand gesture. Marlow didn't move a muscle. His lips were tight, no smirk this time. But his eyes were smiling, as if to say, we are watching you closely, Mr. Wisniewski.

After a continued and extended conversation, Stanley peered out the window of the cabin. He gazed at the expanse of the Mojave Desert below. They were beginning their final descent into Antelope Valley, the southwestern portion of the Mojave. Stanley watched as the barren high desert came into detail. The area was decorated with a scattered army of Joshua trees, all laying prostrate to the San Gabriel Mountains further south. The relative motion of the business jet made them appear to be searching the desert's scrub emptiness for a treasure most desired, but long lost.

Marlow started, "We'll be coming into Palmdale pretty soon. If you look to the north, you should be able to see Edwards Air Force Base. It's just about forty miles to the north. Obviously, our flight plan doesn't allow us to get too close, but you never know what you might see flying over it."

Stanley squinted out the cabin window, but could make out only the mountains and desert.

Marlow interjected, "Last trip out this way, we heard Edwards had a MiG 15 up in the airspace, but we never did get eyes on it."

Stanley could see how the Aerospace lifestyle was alluring to these executives. They could be intoxicated by it, he thought. The higher the level, the more transfixed they could become.

Marlow continued, "There's also a head in the back, just past the sofa, if you care to freshen up before we land."

Stanley decided to forgo the sightseeing and take advantage of this last access before landing. At his age, one did not pass on these opportunities.

Chapter Four

STANLEY FOUND HIMSELF in the business jet's head, somewhat hunched over. His six-foot frame was a contraction of the 6-foot-3 he had been through most of his life, and yet it was still a challenge against the tapering fuselage.

He looked into the mirror into the eyes he had hoped had not betrayed him by looking tired or nervous. He splashed water on his face and looked deeper. He hoped he was strong enough for all this. This was his last great opportunity. He had thought it would never come. Now that it had come, he needed to grasp it.

The seconds stretched into an eternity. Stanley thought again of his father, years earlier, on his deathbed. Their conversation had continued the next day after a somewhat restless night by his father.

"I know you are strong, my Stashew. I hear it in your voice."

"Father, you are incredibly strong, look at all you have been through," replied Stanley

"Stanislaus, I am a weak shell of what I once was. That was a very, very long time ago." Stanley heard him say in his labored, whispered Polish.

"I was strong when I went to University in Krakow. I was there when the invasion came in September 1939. The Germans were everywhere, but Krakow had not suffered physically in the manner that Warsaw had during the invasion in 1939 and through 1940. I just wanted to finish my schooling. I was very skilled in languages, as you now are, Stashew. I was proud and quick to show off my skills in German and Russian. I learned to wish I had never opened my mouth in these tongues."

What color had returned to his ashen face overnight had drained as quickly as these words escaped him.

"I was raised in Poznan in the West of Poland, where speaking German was not unusual. This area had been taken by the Prussians and the Germans over the centuries. But my real skill was in my ability to quickly pick up the Russian language. I was taught by an emigre from Saint Petersburg who lived in the village very close to us. My mind craved to learn all I could."

Stanley recalled the effort his father expended just to get this all out of him. It was as if something was driving him, as if the lack of time had caused him to bare his soul to his 30-year-old son.

"Poznan then was wonderful. A land of beautiful, rich fields of grass, brushed ever so gently by the fingers of the summer's breeze. It is a smell of childhood I have never forgotten. I remembered how I missed it when I went to Krakow for my studies in 1938. This was my first trip to a major, if not medieval, city. I was in Krakow, relatively safe, when the Blitzkrieg invasion from the West was launched in September 1939. Soon the Nazis rounded up all the faculty of the university and deported them to labor camps."

"I survived throughout 1940 as a guest in the home of a kind Krakow family. There were rumors of the University re-opening, but these were only rumors. The Germans had no intention to educate the Poles. They had other plans for us."

"Then in late summer of 1941, we were seated at what had long been a cafe along the boulevard near the Jagiellonian University. There was no service, because the Germans had been hoarding everything, so there was near nothing left for the Polish people in Krakow, or for that matter, anywhere in Poland."

"Six of us were sitting there talking, discussing the situation, as we did often. We couldn't fight back, but we could sharpen our wits for survival. The life we had known was now gone. Germany had just double crossed Russia and launched a surprise invasion of the Soviet Union. Hitler had realized he could not take England from the air, so millions of Germans had just invaded from what had been Poland to get at the Russian homeland."

"Operation Barbarossa." Stanley recalled silently.

His father found the strength to go on. "The Nazis were making incredible gains, taking large numbers of Russians prisoner. Rumors were that the Germans were committing crimes against the Russian people as well as the Russian soldiers. Rumors of many atrocities persisted, even then."

"One of our group of six was my friend from Poznan, who had come to Krakow with me three years earlier. He was Tadeusz Pniewski. We had known each other since we were children in Poznan. We played together, grew together. We went to University together. We were both housed by the same family in Krakow. Poznan, was actually part of German Prussia, during the Partitions of Poland that preceded the first World War. Poznan had become the German city of Posen. But despite Poland having been literally carved off the map for over 120 years, the Polish culture survived."

"Classes at the universities were non-existent because so many of the professors and academics had been arrested by the Germans. Nearly two hundred had been rounded up by the Germans, and we thought taken to the woods and shot. Only years later, did I find out that they had been taken to the Sachsenhausen camp outside of Berlin."

"The University was closed by the Germans shortly thereafter for the first time since it was permanently opened in the year 1400 by Casmir the Great. Even the Austrians did not close it when they partitioned Poland."

"Then the Germans on that beautiful, late summer day moved in to arrest us. Imagine us, simple students, being a threat to them, because they thought we might organize a resistance. This would later prove to become their worst nightmare. They feared that the innocent would become the defiant. They came for us that afternoon."

Stanley remembered watching his father rest for a few minutes, drawing his strength to recall the pain of this part of his life.

"We sat at a stone ledge that had once been part of the cafe. The trees along the boulevard edged the park that fronted the University. They were green and pleasant in the late summer breeze. I remember the mottled shadows of the trees in full bloom cast upon the sidewalks. What had been a peaceful day in wartime was about to be pierced by the crackle of gunfire. It marked the beginning of the end of my life and my soul."

His father wheezed out a half breath, as if stunned by the emotion of recollection, but found his strength and continued on.

"A German military truck pulled up onto the sidewalk. We were all shocked, no one thought to run. After all, we had merely been talking. They pointed their rifles and machine guns at us, herding us into the flat bed of the truck, along with the ten or so other Poles who were already there. As they were approaching us, I could hear the leader saying in German to the soldiers 'Grab them, they will do.' We were later told in Polish by a translator that we were being arrested for conspiracy against the Nazi Party and German Third Reich. The officer's uniform was different from the rest of the soldiers in the truck. It bore a collar patch of a skull. He was SS. Even worse, he was SS Totenkopf."

Stanley knew Totenkopf literally meant skull in German. It went back to the middle ages as a sign of fear and terror, and this division of Hitler's SS was by far the most notorious, and specifically responsible for attacks on the Jews, intelligentsia and political leaders in Poland and elsewhere. Stanley assumed his father was describing his being rolled up in a lower-level, intelligentsia sweep.

"Soon the truck was heading toward the train station adjoining the park square. The SS officer was in the truck bed with all of us and two guards. He spotted a group of four young men gathered near the station, and again in German, I heard the leader yell briskly 'those four, quickly'."

"This time, as the truck pulled up, everyone resisted. They began to scuffle with the German soldiers. A pistol shot rang out. One of the four fell clutching his chest, blood everywhere."

"In all this confusion, Tadeusz grabbed my arm and whispered urgently 'come, now' in Polish. He was going over the side of the truck, only then did I realize that the guards had all left us during the disturbance. Yes, they were only several feet away from the truck, but on the opposite side from where Tadeusz was jumping over. I was frozen in fear and confused. I told him no, but he wouldn't listen. He was determined to take advantage of the German's momentary lapse of attention."

"He began to run to the park, thinking he had not been seen, that the truck was blocking him from the Germans."

"It was the SS officer who spotted him first. He grabbed the arm of the nearest soldier and told him—I can still hear him saying it in German— 'He is escaping. Shoot him, kill him, quick.' I yelled out 'no,' and the SS officer glanced sharply at me, realizing I understood his German. That second froze in the air between us. I had revealed myself to him. That first look cut through my very soul, saying, 'You dare defy me - you and I have unfinished business'."

"The soldier raised his rifle as Tadeusz was rapidly closing in on the largest willow tree in the park. Another few seconds and he would be behind it, giving cover to his escape. I heard the first shot ring out, and looked to see Tadeusz still running, a chunk of the tree exploding just beyond his head. My nerves were so tight I could not breathe. The crackle of the gunfire shot through me like a lightning strike."

"The German soldier dropped his aim slightly. The pause seemed to linger forever, as Tadeusz neared the willow. Only seconds now and he would be beyond it, obscured by its beautiful, massive trunk. Just then a second shot rang out, and Tadeusz immediately stumbled. Off balance he took two more steps before his form dropped to the earth. It was as if he was denying the reality of the round from the carbine that had pierced his chest. He now lay gasping, dying just beneath the willow's bend."

"The SS man walked very deliberately to the scene under the willow. He drew his Luger pistol and pointed it at Tadeusz's head. Tadeusz was in shock, bleeding very badly from the rifle shot through his chest. The officer said something I could not make out over the distance, and squeezed off two shots directly into my young friend's head. I felt such a sorrow, a horror wash over me and drain me of my life senses. It was as if my entire being was razor wire, which had been pulled through my throat, and jammed tightly into my heart. I cried outright. I sobbed, I heaved. I could not believe it was happening."

Young Stanley watched his dying father, ashamed with tears at the thought of his childhood friend lying executed. The tears were less than Stanley had expected. They only rinsed statically in his eyes, like a reflecting pool in a forest stream. Stanley could only assume there was much more in his father's life that drew his tears than just this recollection. Little did Stanley know that no matter how dramatic, Tadeusz' execution was but the opening of a torrent of death his father would live to witness.

His father continued, "The SS officer walked back towards us. Tadeusz's body lay sacrificed in the gentle shade of the willow. Her long strands of leaves dancing in the summer breeze, as if not knowing enough to bow down and mourn the loss of life under its expanse. The tragedy was now marked by an expanding pool of blood in the dirt surrounding Tadeusz's still, lifeless body."

"The SS officer walked briskly back to the truck. Even from the distance he did not take his eyes from my crying, heaving form. He closed the gap to the truck in long, efficient strides that seemed to celebrate his kill."

"The SS officer climbed back in the truck, and worked his way over to me. He said in German, 'Your friend is dead because of you. You told him to run, but you were too scared to join him. You speak German well, eh, perhaps this will keep you alive for a little bit longer. But remember, you Slavic dog, I can kill you like I killed your friend any time I desire'."

"With this he drew his Luger from his holster and raised it to my temple. I tried to withhold my tears, but this only caused me to heave involuntarily."

"Despite my flood of tears, I remember very clearly seeing his thumb release the safety as he raised the gun to my head. It was a momentary sight that has stuck with me for all the moments of my life."

"He stood as close as he could to my sobbing face. His face was like stone, his eyes were cold, black slates. They were staring into my eyes, my eyes that were already red from sobbing openly for Tadeusz."

"He lowered the pistol and broke off from his stare abruptly. As he turned from my view, I sensed an open pleasure soften his face. His jaw relaxed. I sensed he had enjoyed the kill. He was pleased that he had intimidated me."

"He pounded on the roof of the truck's cab, and we were off. It became clear the collections were finished and we were being taken to the western country. I cried knowing we were being taken to the woods to be shot. Had it only been that simple."

Chapter Five

THE CAR WAS waiting for the business jet to finish its taxi on the tarmac at the end of one of Air Force Site 42's 12,000 foot runways in Palmdale. These were shared by multiple Aerospace firms. Lockheed's fabled Skunkworks lay at one end, Northrop Grumman's plant at another. Boeing a third, and the Global Defense Analytics plant, producing the drones, on the final leg of the airstrip.

Stanley's bag was loaded into the car's trunk. They took a short ride to the plant. Marlow stayed out of view on the jet, which refueled and soon headed to DC, to drop him off there before the aircraft returned to its hangar in Baltimore.

Stanley soon found himself in the security office at the Aerospace plant to be registered and badged. The process took longer than the car ride in from the plane itself.

Amazingly, thanks to the early departure and expedited routing, as well as a three-hour time change in his favor, Stanley joined up with the INAR team well before noon.

The head of the team, Bob Moretti, a vice president from the Space Systems segment of the team, welcomed Stanley, introducing him as Howard Burnett's outside consultant of financial risk management.

Stanley had gone over the names and positions of the dozen or so members on the INAR team. He was concerned most about the four members with financial backgrounds. As fate would have it, they tended to steer clear of him, concerned he would ask in-depth financial questions they either wouldn't want to, or couldn't answer. In fact, in the world of corporate Aerospace, it was not uncommon to not engage with outside third parties. Especially when they were brought in by the CFO. It would be one thing for a financial VP to get himself in a bad way with Corporate, but even worse if they got their bosses on an uneven keel. This worked to Stanley's benefit.

The team had been in place since Monday, and as today was now Wednesday, they had done significant fact-finding already. The general assessment was that the proposal being submitted was well-prepared, with only minor findings so far. This would give Stanley the benefit of cover with a minimum of work required for the team itself. Given everyone else on the team were from different business segments of the firm, and Stanley was an outsider, it stood to reason to the team that his debrief would be to Howard Burnett himself.

As Stanley was listening to the debriefs by the Finance, Engineering, Supply Chain and Legal review teams, Moretti came over and asked him to step out of the reviews for a second.

"Langston Powell would like to meet with you at six PM today in his office. He had a Monday evening meeting with the entire INAR team, and spent nearly two hours with us. Seemed to know everyone's background coming in. But given that you are just now joining the team, his office called this morning asking us to free you up at six PM. I know this makes a long day for you coming in from the East Coast, but I told them of course."

"Yes, that won't be problem," replied Stanley. "As long as someone can get me to his office."

"Sure, no problem. Langston is not here in Palmdale. His office is at our corporate headquarters in Irvine close to the John Wayne Airport. But they've arranged for the company shuttle to fly you over the mountains. There will be other executives on board – this thing flies back and forth several times a day. Bad news is you will have to be driven back as this is the last shuttle of the day, and given the traffic you likely won't be back until ten PM or so."

"Not a problem. I'll just take my bag and spend the night at the closest Marriott. I can fly back on the morning shuttle," Stanley replied.

"Stanley, I really don't know what access you are going to need. Financial Risk Management covers a lot of territory, and I need for you to let me know which aspects of this proposal you wish to dive deeper into," Moretti said.

"Well, that pretty much makes both of us at this point, but before this team winds up next week, I should be able to let you know what areas I want to focus on." Stanley was now trying to be as general as possible, with only minimum specifics peppered in. "Certainly, I want to assess the stability of the supply chain, once your engineering team tells me we have a stable design. Also, I would like to review the executive financial and program leadership, perhaps interview them, to assure we are not spreading the existing leadership too thin."

Moretti responded, "OK, I figured something along those lines. Well, for the rest of the day listen to the team debriefs—the proposal volumes are over on the table. We have been asked not to let them leave this room, especially the pricing volumes. But feel free to take them over to your seat as needed. Most of the rest of the team have been through them Monday and yesterday. I'll come by and escort you to the shuttle at about quarter to five."

So, Stanley did exactly that, poured through the proposal itself, starting with the requirements decomposition section, the disciplined process used to assure each requirement set forth in the government's Request For Proposal, or RFP, was adequately addressed. He started here because it would give him a working knowledge of the proposal the fastest, and at least allow him to elaborate upon areas he intended to dive deeper into for his cover story. He did this while listening intently to the team debriefs.

Lunch was brought in to the team conference room, and the rigor of the morning sessions loosened up as everyone grabbed a box lunch and soft drink. As Stanley opened his lunch, he struck up a casual conversation with the INAR Engineering team lead, who sat next to him.

Lou Cerilla was in rolled-up shirt sleeves, revealing the bottom of a tattoo that Stanley could not distinguish. Unusual for this crowd.

"So I understand you all had a two-hour session with Langston Powell Monday evening," Stanley opened.

"Yeah, after traveling on our own time Sunday evening, he keeps us here until nearly 8 o'clock Monday night. What a host," said Cerilla, the head of Engineering from the Missiles Business Area, the same Business Area that Langston Powell originally came from. "And all the time we have the *distinction* of being on this team, my own work is piling up back east. It's a great gig, can't wait for the next week and a half to be over."

"Come on, Lou," another voice chirped in. "It's not that bad. At least

Mr. Powell flew up from Irvine. Besides, I kind of like being the inquisitors for a change. God knows I have to put up with enough of these INAR teams back in Space Systems." The voice was Guy Grossman, also Engineering.

"Yeah, I don't mind asking the questions for a change," responded Cerilla. "But we really didn't get much of a chance to do that Monday night, did we? Langston hasn't changed a bit since he was at Missiles – all T no R."

"What does that mean?" Stanley failed to get the reference.

Grossman jumped in, "Lou means Powell was all Transmit, no Receive. But at least he gave us some significant time with him. How often do you get a president of a Business Area for two hours?"

"That was a dose I could have done without," Lou Cerilla responded. "For two hours hearing 'I created this algorithm, I came up with the guidance system on that missile, I fixed this aircraft's software problems.' For God's sake, the guy will look you in the eye and tell you he created air."

"What was the problem with the drone's software? Is that a problem we are likely to have on this proposal?" Stanley was fishing now.

Cerilla snorted, "Hey, let me tell you something, I was on that corporate tiger team under Ted Barber that fixed the Daedalus Destroyer software, and Langston baby didn't have anything to do with it. He only came onto the program as we were wrapping up."

Stanley could see the other faces were rolling their eyes. They could see Cerilla was just getting spun up.

"In fact, that really pissed me off the other night, because Barber and I were the heavy lifters on that team. Look where it got Ted, edged out, exiled and now permanently out of the game. The big permanent."

Grossman was more delicate in his response, attempting to answer the question directly. Little did he know that Cerilla was providing the insights Stan was looking for. Grossman was more polished than Cerilla, and certainly more considerate. His complexion was reddish pale to Cerilla's Latin dark coloring. They might as well have been night and day.

Grossman responded, "To answer your question, Stan, Daedalus Destroyer had a unique issue, to a point. All of its software, its data communications, the propulsion controls and the flight controls – the control of the leading edges, the ailerons, the rudders – were all balled up in a single immense segment of code. It was what's called an integrated software build. Made it extremely hard to troubleshoot when the jet's software was crashing every couple of minutes, requiring resets."

"Yeah, these drones aren't crazy about flying blind while the software was rebooting." It was Cerilla again. "These things are called Daedalus Destroyers because when they work they leave the bad guys 'dead-or-less.' But when that software is rebooting they don't destroy nothing, don't fly very well and under certain conditions fire off missiles randomly."

"Fired missiles randomly?" Stanley was amazed.

"Sure as shit. Software gets so balled up that sometimes these bad boys don't realize they just fired off a round over Yemen or Afghanistan."

"Don't listen to him. That kind of thing is very rare," stated Grossman, trying to stay out of ancient history that posed no current risk.

Grossman then went on to provide the definition Cerilla so care-lessly omitted. "It's likely that it was their inability to collect data that caused everyone to get the most annoyed, back in the day. There could be no electronic sweep and data collection while the system rebooted, which could take up to two minutes, during which they were controlled by an autonomous flight control routine, while the rest of the operating system was reloaded."

"So this version of drone program won't have this problem?" Stanley inquired.

"No, that was fixed by Barber and his team a while back," Guy an-swered. "The various systems are now all federated, meaning distinct blocks of code for each function. Makes it a lot easier to trouble-shoot unexpected errors in the code. And don't listen to Lou about uncommanded missile launches. That's a myth created by the anti-drone community."

"I should hope so. So why would any program ever undertake an integrated system software approach, then?"

"Because they fell for the myth of less lines of code," Cerilla started, this time with a quarter of his sandwich in his mouth. "The idiots went hook, line, and sinker for the myth of saving about 20% of the SLOCS (Guy later explained this stood for software Source Lines of Code) on the jet. Which meant there would be room to add more functions on the jet later. In reality, when we started digging into that code, there was so much spaghetti in there that they would have saved 20% going Federated from the get-go."

"Spaghetti?" Stanley was now playing a little dumb, just to keep

Cerilla going.

"Yeah, this subroutine calls out that subroutine, which then calls out a third. Everybody putting in their little 'efficient' calls to other parts of the software. Only problem is there were about thirty major coders on that software, and most of their documentation was shit."

Cerilla went on, having choked down the food before reloading. "There is no way I am allowing that to happen again on this proposal, absolutely no way. That is where my ass is focused for the next ten days. I'll be diving so deep on that team that they're going to feel like its annual physical time. And I'll be the one with the rubber gloves."

"Good God, Lou, how'd you ever get to be a VP with a mouth like that," Guy Grossman said with an incredible look on his pallid face.

"They ain't paying me for playing nice, Guy," Lou answered. "They're paying me to keep them out of trouble and get the job done. And don't suck up all that uncommanded launch-is-a-myth shit. Remember, I was on that team."

The afternoon briefings were underway later, and Stanley was pouring through the financial volume for reference. The afternoon became a monotone, death-by slide show, blurred together with the broad strokes of the financial proposal. But one thing was for sure, the profit margins on these drones was significantly higher than typical military programs. Stanley felt that because these sales were going to the CIA, and not to the Department of Defense, the scrutiny on acquisition was dialed back. Certainly Langston Powell had made his place in Global Defense Analytics through realizing these higher profit margins via the CIA. It was clear there was a lot of money being made in these Daedalus Destroyer drones.

Soon it was quarter to five and Bob Moretti was escorting Stanley to the shuttle aircraft. In less than forty-five minutes, Stanley would be being led through the maze of halls to the executive suite in Irvine.

"You've been crammed up in the conference room all day, at least I can take a slight detour past the Daedalus Destroyer production line," Moretti offered.

"That would be great." Stanley had seen many aircraft production lines over the years, but never a drone line.

Moretti, having detoured them, had them walking along the drone assembly line before accessing the maze of corridors leading to the shuttle aircraft.

The drones lay tip to tail, with each one more complete than the one behind it. Stanley was surprised it was not a moving assembly line, but was told that it really did not work well for complex systems such as a fighter or a drone.

"I have never been so close to a drone aircraft before," Stanley affected. "They are much larger than I ever would have guessed."

"Well, they need to be big," responded Moretti. "They need to carry a fair amount of fuel to stay aloft, and they take a sizable dynamic load when their missiles come off the rails. The bigger the platform, the more stable the separation. That means more weapons on target."

"All without a pilot," Stanley added. "All flying from a joystick?"

"Not these," added Moretti. "Yeah, the guys in the bunkers can take them over, but these fly autonomously, seeking out targets. The only man in the loop is the one who approves the weapons launch in the kill-chain."

"Kill chain? You're kidding?" Stanley was fishing again.

"Not kidding. Today's Concept of Operations, CONOPS in our lingo, call for there to be a man in the kill chain for every shoot. But you should have heard Langston Powell on Monday night convincing us that we are not far away from having truly autonomous drones flying themselves while constantly making decisions on who to launch weapons against. This is the vision of the guy who earlier in his career wrote the autonomous piloting code that is used today. First drones, then unmanned fighters will be next. Won't be long before we have fully autonomous weapons in the skies. From listening to Langston Powell the other night, he is looking forward to selling a lot of these to our government, and anybody else Washington will allow him to."

That thought scared the hell out of Stanley. He was smart enough to see the many abuses, domestically and abroad.

"So I heard you got to meet Lou and Guy at lunch this afternoon. I was out making calls or I would have introduced you," Moretti continued.

"Well, they were both great. Guy Grossman appears to be very disciplined, very methodical," said Stanley.

"Yes, and Lou is a brilliant engineer also," Moretti jumped in, "But sometimes his irreverence gets in his way. He likes to be critical of Langston as they both came up through the ranks together, and Lou gets a little riled that Langston has left him in the executive dust. Langston is big time now, and if rumors are right he is in line for a major Corporate posting soon. Lou can see him ending up in the CEO seat and it drives him crazy."

"What about you, do you see Powell going that far?" Stanley prompted.

"Well, you know, ability is the entrance ticket for the senior executive ranks," Bob responded. "After you make it into that club, it really is all about positioning yourself for the next promotion. And they get fewer and the competition gets considerably better the higher one goes. So he who boxes out his competition wins, and it is clear that Langston Powell does that very well."

"Does that make him ruthless?" Stanley asked, putting Moretti on the spot.

"Well, that question is best answered by the trail of people he has beaten out along the way. I suspect Cerilla was one of them back in the day. It would explain a lot of Lou's sour grapes. But Langston has a long history of getting his way."

Stanley noticed Bob's volume was dropping more and more to a soft whisper as they approached people in the halls. Some things are best not overheard.

Suddenly, the halls opened to a small glass lobby that opened onto the tarmac. A golf cart would take Stanley to the Turbo prop and a very bumpy ride over the California mountains.

A representative from the president's office was waiting at the other end to escort Stanley to Langston Powell. Soon they were pulling open the glass doors into the large expansive room. This was more of an executive visitor's center oversized with four red leather sofas paired off in twos in the center. Along the four walls were positioned the administrative assistants for all the Executive VP's of the Aerospace Leadership. Behind each of them were their individual offices, which Stanley assumed were nicely appointed, but nothing to the level of Marc Constantine's retirement office from the morning before.

To get to Langston's office, one had to pass to the other end of the room through a second set of etched glass doors announcing the entrance to the office of the President of Aerospace. The administrative assistant had waived Stanley right through into Langston Powell's private office, passing a cluster of three financial directors on their way out of Powell's office from the meeting just ending. Their faces were visibly reddened, they looked displeased. "Must have been a tough meeting," Stanley thought.

Powell didn't waste a second, standing up from behind his desk to welcome Stanley. His face was still transitional–still flush from the previous meeting, but now smoothing into a broad, forced smile.

"Come in," Powell smiled. He was trim, fit and commanding in only his suit pants and dress shirt. Cuff links, of course. Striped tie on a yet more finely striped shirt. Stanley would never wear it, but Langston Powell pulled it off.

"You must be Stanley _Vish–nev–ski_." Polish pronunciation perfect. "_Yak se mash?_" Powell asked, as he shook Stanley's hand firmly. His Polish pronunciation was pure butchery of "how are you" in Polish - _Jak się masz_ - but Stanley appreciated the gesture.

"Yes, thank you, Mr. Powell. I am very well, thanks," Stanley responded. It was a phrase everyone tried on you when they found out you were Polish. Stanley decided to have a little fun, breaking back into Polish, "_Czy pan mówi po polsku?_"

"Whoa, Stanley," laughed Langston heartily. "You just got everything I had. So what did you just say?"

"Just asking if you spoke Polish," Stanley continued. "Your pronunciation was that good," he teased.

"Testing me, Stanley? Really, we just met." Langston's smile broke the sharp edge of his words.

"Do you really speak Polish? I mean fluently?" Langston inquired. Not waiting for a response, he added, "I am headed over to Poznan next week to meet with the Polish government on a potential business arrangement regarding maintaining their existing systems. Could be able to lay the groundwork for a new missile defense system sale while I'm there. Might be nice to have someone with your skills along."

"Actually, my family is originally from a small town just outside of Poznan." Stanley stated incidentally.

"But you were born here in the states?" Powell asked.

"Yes, in late '45. My parents were lucky to have gotten out before the Iron Curtain fell. A lot of my family was left behind."

Stanley felt comfortable with Powell, something he didn't expect.

"Well, some of us boys from Tennessee could never relate to the environment you grew up in. But here we are, all from meager beginnings, no royalty that I am aware of," Langston said, his broad smile flowing into hearty laughter.

The guide who dropped Stanley off was standing awkwardly in the door.

"Mr. Powell, do you want me to wait for Mr. Wisniewski to drop him at his hotel?" The young man announced Stanley's name in the anglicized "*Wiz New Ski*" fashion.

Langston jumped in before Stanley could. "Ted, Ted, you just butchered Stanley's name. In Polish there is no V, so the W's make a V sound. Stanley's name is *Vish NEV Ski*, not *Wiz New Ski*. The second syllable is always emphasized. I have done enough work with the Poles to tell you they get insulted if you don't make the effort to pronounce their names correctly."

Stanley's hair was standing up on the back of his neck. Was this really from his business dealings or was this leaked to Powell? Powell cocked his neck and looked at Stanley with a warm, toying smile, as if to say "impressed"?

Ted was now flustered. "Sorry, sir, I didn't realize. I was just going by the pronunciation of the Wisniewski players I see in professional football."

"Not a big deal, Ted. I am used to it." Stanley let him off the hook.

"But you do prefer *Vis-nev-ski*, Stanley?" Powell interrupted forcibly. He had to be right, which he was, of course.

"Yes, actually I prefer the Polish pronunciation, Mr. Powell," Stanley conceded.

"Oh, please, call me Langston, no need for Mr. Powell. I'll be looking for my Dad to pop out of the background somewhere." At this, Ted took his cue to leave them both alone and wait in the outer office.

"Is Stanley, OK? Would you prefer Stanislaus, or even Stash?" Powell grinned at him. Stanley felt he was being mocked to a point.

"Stanley is fine, thank you."

"So, how do you know Howard? I am surprised our paths haven't crossed before. Usually I know all of Howard's tricks, but pulling in a high level consultant into an INAR, I have never seen him do that before."

"I have done some work for Mr. Burnett here and there. He just asked for my input on this team. I am sorry I wasn't able to be here with the rest of the team on Monday."

"Oh don't worry about that, Stanley," Powell said, sitting back in his chair behind the desk, crossing his legs. Stanley sat across the desk. The conference table behind Stanley remained unused. Stanley took this as Langston reminding him who had the power.

"Damn shame about Sally Burnett," Langston said, his face now taut with sincerity. Now it appeared it was Powell's turn to test Stanley.

"I do not know Howard's family. Is that his wife? In fact, I have spent very little time with Howard himself. I am just a hired analyst, I must confess." Stanley answered openly but guardedly.

"Well, Howard must have a lot of faith in you to send you here. So, Financial Risk Management. What exactly does that entail, Stanley? Pretty broad area, isn't it? Could cover a lot of waterfront, that term."

Langston wasted no time at all.

"Typically, I assess the Financial Risk Triggers. In this case, they could be maturity of the design – software maturity, let's say - as well as the ability of the supply chain to support the build rate. Also, the risk of concurrently testing the derivative design while the production drones are being built. I then assign a risk factor to each of these areas, and your teams will address any areas that we deem to be of moderate risk. High risk areas will be an entirely different discussion, if there are any."

"Fair enough, Stanley. I think you'll find my team has these areas sufficiently covered. I've been over most of this with them. I think you will be very satisfied."

"I am sure you have them focused on all the right areas," Stanley responded. "I look forward to next week's out brief."

"Stanley, I really do need to go to Poznan early next week. I was going to have my Operations VP stand in for me in the debrief. I wasn't kidding about dragging you to Poznan, and then I was going to go on to Warsaw. We are seriously looking into expanding our international office there in addition to the operations in Poznan. Have you been to Warsaw?"

"Yes, of course," said Stanley, "many times." If only Powell knew Warsaw had been Stanley's posting for most of his professional career.

"Great," said Powell. "You can show me around a little. Get me acclimated to the culture. Since I have taken this job I have been to Poznan several times, but I have only been through the Warsaw airport and never seen any of the sights. I hear it is very beautiful since the Poles rebuilt it after the war."

"Yes. It is very beautiful. The Old Town was rebuilt brick for brick after the Germans destroyed it in retaliation for the Polish resistance uprising of 1944. I would love to show you around, but I am engaged on this assignment for Mr. Burnett."

"Oh, don't you worry about that," Powell dismissed, playfully flexing his thick fingers of his oversized hands. "I'll talk to Howard and get it all squared away. Perhaps we can extend your contract with Howard, for simplicity to cover this. God knows with the flow down I am paying to Corporate, I'm paying for it already."

"Very well. As it stands I have my passport with me. I do not like to travel without it, exactly for situations like this," Stanley added.

"So you have done business in Poland? Is that how you are so familiar with Warsaw?" Powell was now testing him directly.

"No, more recreational than that. I enjoy vacationing there, visiting distant relatives, using my Polish." Stanley, of course, would not mention his operational assignments there for the Agency.

"Well, it won't hurt to have a Polish translator with me in Poznan. Maybe we'll catch onto something we should know. With this international business, knowledge is leverage."

Stanley now decided to go on the offensive somewhat. "Speaking of international business, I was sorry to see your internal release on the death of your International Office Vice President, Mr. Barber, this past weekend."

"Did you know, Ted?" Powell reacted. His face looked surprised that this would come up.

"No. I merely saw your release today and heard others discussing it at lunch."

"Well, I knew Ted Barber very well. He worked for me as we matured the Daedalus Destroyer design. As it turns out I was with him in London late last week, and I flew from there to Amsterdam on Saturday to have dinner with him. I was trying to get him to come join my team here in California. But Ted had some issues, and I am afraid they finally caught up with him."

"I am sorry, I thought he was found drowned in the canal," Stanley probed.

"How does one end up in a canal, drowned? Drunk? Foul play? Maybe he was visiting someone he shouldn't have been. Who knows? People just don't fall into canals in Amsterdam every night. I am sure the police will sort it out," Powell said unworried. He seemed not disturbed by the discussion in the least.

The game had begun.

Stanley waited a second to let Langston's comment settle. "I see. There was something else I would like to ask, if I may. I was curious how the Daedalus Destroyer got its name?"

"Well, Stanley, I am surprised a worldly man such as yourself doesn't know his Greek mythology," Powell started. "Daedalus was the father of Icarus, and he was the master artisan that created the wings for them both to escape their island imprisonment."

Stanley hesitated, then added, "Yes. That's what confused me. When Icarus flew too close to the sun, his wings melted and he was drowned in the sea. Daedalus, having watched his son drown due to the work of his own hands, forever regretted having crafted the wings."

Powell's face went rigid. Stanley saw in his expression an edge he had not seen earlier, as it was masked by Powell's joviality. He saw a flash of anger on being audaciously quizzed by an outsider he did not know. Powell contained his temper, but his response was now forcibly strained.

"Very interesting, Stanley. But we have no regrets about creating this technology, Stan. The Daedalus Destroyer is here to stay." He peered into Stanley's eyes, unrelenting. "And our country will be all the safer for having them."

Chapter Six

STANLEY FOUND HIMSELF at the hotel later that evening. He was exhausted after his extended day. He stretched out on his bed in his clothes, listening to Chopin in the earphones from his outdated but still functioning CD portable player. No iPod, no music on his mobile phone. He was comfortable with his CD player, and its music soothed him and cleared his mind. As the familiar piano's crystalline falsetto danced in his ears, he closed his eyes and thought about the already long day.

He thought about his father. He listened to the deathbed oratory of his father continue over the strains of a beautifully somber Chopin nocturne.

"We were being forcibly taken to the town of Oświęcim, about 50 kilometers northwest of Krakow. I had known this country, as I had ridden on the train through it from Katowice to Krakow. But as the truck plowed through the country roads we passed many villagers from Oświęcim who had been displaced by the Nazis. They wandered, not really sure where they would go or what their families would do. They had been driven from their land and their homes. The Nazis had need for their farms, modest as they be, so they took them. The villagers dared not resist. They were lost."

"We were driven on the truck through the vacated buffer lands to the camp that the Nazis had taken from the Polish Army. Only it was clear that it had been undergoing a large expansion. So this is where I would die, I thought. This is where I have been brought to be shot, away from prying eyes."

"Stashew, we were unloaded from the truck. The SS man had the twenty or so of us line up for what I was later to find out was called 'the selection'. But it was clear that we had been pre-selected from before we entered the truck. They were looking for laborers, and what better way to clear out some students in the same effort."

"The Nazis feared the country's intelligentsia, that it would form the core of the Polish resistance itself. And they were right in doing so. So, I had been taken because the Nazis needed labor to expand this camp. I would soon learn it was the first of many expansions."

"In the selection, we were paraded in front of other SS officers and asked simple questions, 'How old are you? Are you healthy? Do you have any skills?'"

"When I was confronted with the last question, the SS officer from the truck responded in German to the inquisitor that I spoke excellent German. He had never actually heard me speak German at that point, but was playing to his superiors the value of the catch he had made. The inquisitor than asked me in German if I this was true. I answered that it was, and that I was also proficient in Russian. This appeared to catch the attention of the inquisitor, as he looked approvingly to the SS officer who had rounded us up.

"I was told to move to the right. Most of us were, as we had been pre-selected. But of the twenty or so of us, three were told to move to the left. They were condemned to die, and were later shot dead. We were forced to witness this. I assume to teach us a lesson."

"I had thought many times about that moment. It was not unusual for some Poles to be proficient in German or Russian, especially given that the country had been divided between Austria and Prussia in the West, and Russia in the East before World War I. The fact that I was proficient in Polish, German and Russian meant I had a certain level of utility to the Nazis. Especially in this camp. Over the next several years I would wish I didn't have these skills, as they were the sentence that kept me from the release of death."

"We were soon standing in front of the main gate leading into the red brick barracks, five abreast. Above the head of another SS officer in front of us arched a metallic sign that read '*Arbeit Macht Frei*,' German for '*Work Sets You Free*.' It was the first of their lies, except in the sense that when one could no longer work he was freed by death."

"Perhaps this is what they meant, perhaps they found a sick humor in this," the young Stanley thought, not interrupting his father. He could see his father crying again. His father's voice wobbled on the razor's edge of control.

His father continued, "The camp was being used to collect the overflow of Poles from the regional prisons. With the roundup of the intelligentsia and government and religious leadership of Poland, there was no more room. The Jews were still at this time being mostly restricted to the ghettos of Warsaw, Krakow and Lodz. But at the time I was brought there, there already was a steady infusion of another group – Red Army soldiers captured once Hitler betrayed his Russian allies and attacked eastward earlier that summer."

"At the camp, the SS officers scowled from a raised platform down onto us. The leader began, 'You have been brought here to this camp in Auschwitz' - the Germans had renamed what was left of the town of Oświęcim - 'because you have been found guilty of conspiring against the Third Reich. But you have an option to regain your freedom through hard work. This is a labor camp. You will serve your sentence here performing tasks that are difficult and strenuous. But through this you will earn consideration for your future freedom. Today, you will be inducted; tomorrow, you shall work. Be thankful you are not here as the bulk of our prisoners – Soviet Prisoners of War. They are enemy swine and not to be spoken to. You may be shot if observed speaking to them. That is all.'

"I later learned that the first Auschwitz camp – later called Auschwitz I – had been open for nearly a year. It had been expanded from the original sixteen barracks to many more. At this point it had already exceeded ten thousand inmates, mostly Poles and Soviets POWs from the recent German Army press into the Soviet Union. This would come to be dwarfed by the number of Jews from all over Europe who would be brought here, especially after the camp was further expanded to include the dreaded efficiency of Auschwitz II, more infamously known as Birkenau. Here, death would be industrialized beyond what anyone could imagine. It was as if the horror of the beast had been unleashed on mankind."

"Then the twenty or so of us were taken for showers, where we were stripped of our clothes and possessions. We actually had showers, reduced to being naked, stripped of our dignity, in front of those we knew and many more we did not. We were showered *en masse* under very cold water. I remember later the guilt I felt when I witnessed what was done to so many in the guise of these showers. But at this point, that terror had not yet been realized.

"I was treated by the camp guards as subhuman. They constantly referred to us as dogs or swine. We dared not look them in the eyes, for that alone would draw a fierce, savage beating. Over the years that followed, I saw several die from those beatings alone."

"They saw us as animals. No, worse, an infestation of vermin. Perhaps, this is what their minds had to do to justify the terrible pain, suffering and death they inflicted upon us. Perhaps, no mind could reconcile onto itself the brutality we were shown, except to convince itself we were not human."

"But we were men. Men broken of their body and their spirit. My soul and my body began to wither that day, and soon I would have no soul. Just a hollow body, empty, broken, but alive enough to feel only the physical pain of existence. Very soon there was no emotion of any kind. They soon took my soul and killed my God. They numbered me with ink, and branded me like an animal."

"They forced me to live to see the vast majority that were never numbered, just led to the showers directly from the trains."

He closed his eyes, even now, suffering on his deathbed from the images he was forced to bear witness to. Living had been painful for him since that very day in Auschwitz in 1941. In Baltimore, in 1975, he was still alive, and so he suffered still.

Chapter Seven

STANLEY RESTED. HE cleared his mind from the overload of new information, and his body from the weariness of traversing three time zones the day before. The next day he flew back to Palmdale on the shuttle. He immersed himself into the proposal, while continuing to pulse Moretti, Cerilla and Grossman for insight into Langston Powell's personality and relationship with Ted Barber.

The next day flew by in a stream of engineering factors, overhead allowances, and cost substantiations. As Stanley's energy ebbed, the day dragged on into early evening, with Moretti pushing the team to stay on tempo. This all had to be completed before next week, he reminded them. Stanley became conscious of his own task's timeline. He was on day two. Just a week or so to go. In reality, he knew he did not have even that much time.

Moretti drove Stanley to his Palmdale Hotel. Stanley checked in and was glad to finally have someplace to lay his briefcase and bag.

Dinner that night was down the street from the hotel at a modest but authentic game restaurant. Stanley and Bob Moretti met Lou Cerilla and Guy Grossman at the bar. Cerilla picked the restaurant because it offered recipes from game - venison, quail, and the like – flown in from across the country. Cerilla claimed to know the proprietor, an Aerospace Engineer who decided to get out of engineering and into the restaurant business. It was an old but renovated Mexican cantina hailing back to the fifties. Its stucco walls were decorated with private photos of just about every aircraft to have ever flown the well-bored skies of Antelope Valley. Many were signed by test pilots and crew. There were even some legendary ones. It was a very popular diversion in the slim dinner pickings of the high desert. Especially, when one had his fill of Mexican fare and shied away from the national chain restaurants.

After a couple rounds of drinks at the bar, they settled into a nice meal over some very good food in a cozy side dining room off the main dining floor. Stanley ordered a T-Bone steak, the likes of which one could rarely find on the east coast.

Cerilla ordered a grilled elk steak; Grossman, the blackened buffalo ribeye, and Moretti had a cowboy ribeye that he regretted the minute he saw the size of the cut. The conversation flowed freely, having been loosened by the two rounds at the bar and now the two bottles of Bordeaux that Cerilla insisted on having with the meal. The wine was excellent.

Stanley waited until the conversation drifted to Langston Powell, which it inevitably did. Cerilla was the first to get there. "Langston has really shot up the corporate pecking order. He is now one of the top eight officers in the corporation, even after we all thought he was finished after screwing up at missiles."

"What screw up was that?" Stanley probed.

"Oh, you didn't sense Mr. Perfect had a defect hiding in his past did you?" The wine was loosening Cerilla's tongue, a tongue that needed little incentive to wag.

"When Lanny and I were actually doing code for a living, I got called in to clean up a lot of his mess. Seems he had been coding a targeting algorithm for a system being tested at White Sands." Stanley knew this was the missile range at White Sands, New Mexico.

Cerilla continued. "Well, Lanny's work wasn't cutting the mustard. The accuracy wasn't even close to what was needed. I can't go into it because it is all classified, of course, but let's just say I had to spend three months rewriting and testing that code."

"So how did Powell survive that?" Stanley asked.

"By selling my ass down the river. He staged an event with a young female engineer to get her to claim I harassed her in the classified SCIF."

"Skiff?" asked Stanley, playing along.

"Good God, Stanley, how long you been at this? SCIF. Secure Compartmented Information Facility. Haven't you ever been behind doors in a closed area?"

If you only knew, Stanley thought to himself.

"I got a full-blown ethics accusation. Nothing was proven, because there were only three of us in the SCIF at that time. Me, her and the Program Manager who saw nothing from his office. She claimed I groped her. Nothing farther from the truth. God, I wish I hadn't been there. I got raked over the coals, complete with unpaid time off and a threat my career would be over if I ever acted that way again. Hell, she wasn't worth groping in the first place."

Moretti chimed in, "Lou, you're talking too much again..."

"Screw it, Bob. I'm just telling what happened. Stanley's got a right to know what Lanny's really like. Anyway, Stanley, like I said I got time off for good behavior (Lou cracked up at his own joke) and Lanny moved back in, finished up the testing and rode the success all the way to VP. Sold a hell of lot of missiles after I fixed them. I got moved back in line and didn't get my VP until after Lanny left Missiles for Aerospace."

Stanley jumped in with "I'm surprised he was made President of Aerospace after all that."

"Yeah, but that missile program brought a lot of cash into the firm's coffers until the Daedalus Destroyer program got up and approached production," added Grossman. "The profits off the missile production kept the cash coming in, and we all know cash is king. So from that standpoint, having Langston move into the Daedalus Destroyer program manager and later the Aerospace leadership role made perfect sense to those who count the cash."

Cerilla's face was tightening with every positive comment made regarding Powell. He unleashed, "Let me tell you guys about that son of a bitch. I wouldn't trust him with watching my back, not for ten seconds. In fact, he's already got his second jab in on me. I found out from my mentor a couple years later when I was up for my VP appointment, old Lanny went out of his way to say I wasn't VP material, not strategic enough or some bullshit. I got this directly from my guy who was in on the selection panel, and was also told that Lanny got pissed off when his recommendation was over-ridden. I got the appointment anyway. He would gut his mother for his next appointment. Look at what he did to Barber." Lou shoved another hunk of meat into his mouth.

"What did he do to Barber?" Stanley asked, fishing for details.

"When Lanny gets the Aerospace position, Barber could do no wrong, because he was already a golden boy with the team at Corporate. Lanny kept pumping him up, shining up his awards for him, giving him the best assignments. That's how Barber got the Chief Engineer position. Went to Ted's head a little, too." Cerilla was talking through his half-chewed elk steak, which he finally chewed and swallowed.

Lou took a gulp of the Bordeaux and continued unimpeded. "I know all this after working so closely with Barber on the Daedalus Destroyer's software recovery tiger team. Ted thought Lanny was great. As the software got fixed, and Ted got the credit for leading that team, Lanny made him his deputy, and that's when the trouble started. Ted couldn't believe the number Lanny Powell did on his ass."

"Lou, you are getting into rumor and innuendo now," warned Moretti.

"Bullshit, Bob," Cerilla reacted. "Barber used to call me up to cry on my shoulder. He went from favorite son to bastard stepchild over-night. It all started when the drone production got cut way back by the Air Force."

"Corporate wanted to know what the real root cause on this was and Lanny pointed right at Barber and the unnecessary complexity of the systems driving up the per unit cost. Of course, that was all done before Ted ever got there. Ted took the hit. Fact was Lanny didn't want to give up a penny to the Air Force."

"Come on, Lou." Grossman tempered the negativity of the conversation. "Corporate is smart enough to know that no one engineer, even the Chief Engineer, could be singularly responsible for that. "

"Oh, no," challenged Lou. "At this point in your career I thought you would have seen that corporate America loves winners and losers. 'Don't get caught up in the complexity,' they say, 'the best minds are capable of simplifying complex issues'. Well, let me tell you, the best corporate minds are skilled at pinning the blame on someone other than themselves. It's called survival, my friend."

"So you think that was the only reason Powell didn't back Ted to replace him on the drone program?" Moretti asked.

"Lanny got the Daedalus Destroyer production taken over by the CIA when Afghanistan blew-up. The Air Force always hated drones. No plane worth flying could fly without a pilot – so they think. Now the spooks love drones. The fewer bodies the better. The Daedalus proved more capable than the other drones, especially when Lanny claims to have come up with the idea to hang ISR off the drone".

"ISR?" asked Stanley.

"Intelligence, Surveillance, Reconnaissance. Shit, don't they teach you guys anything in MBA school? Think listening and positioning devices," Cerilla barked. "Besides, there was more. Barber told me that he and Powell had a gun battle going on over a technical issue – one he couldn't discuss. I tried to get the info out of him, but he wouldn't go there. My guess is it was classified, and I wasn't read in on it, so Ted wouldn't even hint at it. He was a real stickler on that security stuff."

"Everybody at this table is, aren't we, Lou?" reminded Moretti.

Cerilla's face now crumpled like a used dish rag. "Yeah, yeah, of course. It's just some guys have a skill for telling you something, without really telling you anything, if you get me."

"Lou, I think you're telling us all more than you want. Let's move on," said Moretti firmly.

"So anyway, Barber starts getting frustrated at no more promotions, and starts fooling around on the side, his wife finds out. Bingo, his family throws him out and the next thing you know he's got nobody and nothing, except a cushy job in London."

"So why does corporate put him in that position," Stanley asks.

Lou jumped on the fat pitch over the middle of the plate. "Because Ted went to Powell and told him if he didn't get it, he was going to raise his technical concerns, without saying what they were, with the guys at Corporate. He knew Lanny was deathly afraid of whatever it was, and that it could prevent him from getting or keeping the Aerospace Presidency."

Stanley glanced at the others at the table, whose stares were telling Lou to shut the hell up. He didn't. "So the next thing we all know, Powell is backing Ted for the London Office head spot. And everybody's happy. At least for a while. All directly from Barber's mouth himself. I stopped in and had dinner with him in Covent Garden last time I was in the UK. We were buds."

The conversation continued on other topics and the meal was devoured, as much as it could be. When the second bottle of Bordeaux was polished off completely, Moretti took control.

"Well, gentlemen," Moretti interrupted the now faltering conversation, "It's been a long day, especially for Stan here. I have the check and tip covered. I suggest we call it a night".

And so they did.

The four men drove back to the hotel. Stanley stopped by the front desk to get a 4 AM wake-up call. When it came, Stanley made an international call. It was time to spend some of the information funds Mr. Roberts had so eagerly agreed to supply.

Chapter Eight

"MY STASHEW, COME close," his father whispered.

It was a day later in 1975. His father was as rested as he could get, which means he was merely severely fatigued, instead of the incomprehensibly exhausted state he had been in the night before when they stopped.

"You grew here. On these streets. By this waterfront. You played on the wharves, on the recreation pier. You went to school at Saint Stanislaus Elementary School around the corner. It was a good neighborhood. The Polish people here were good. This was my only hope, for you to have a good childhood. It is why I left Poland to come here where you could grow and have opportunities."

Stanley remembered the Polish neighborhood of his youth in East Baltimore in the fifties and sixties. Where it was not uncommon to have conversations in Polish in the Broadway Market, or in Siemek's butcher shop, or at any number of other establishments. Polish was taught at Saint Stanislaus. It was a good place to be raised.

"But my son, first I had to survive. I was in Auschwitz for three years, from the summer of 1941 until the summer of 1944. Had I known it would have been that long, I would have never made it.

It was hell in the flesh. Everyone there sacrificed their souls. Most sacrificed their lives. Very few survived for as long as I did. Very few, only a handful, if that."

"Once you let your soul go, you can never get it back, my son. They took it all. Your name, your life, your religion, your soul. All you have left is your memories. They leave those to torture you for the rest of your existence. Once you let your soul go, you do not live any longer, you merely exist."

"My young strong body withered away rapidly. Black watery coffee in the morning, even more watery soup in the afternoon, and a scrap of bread. This is what they expected us to live on, or more likely to die from. They treated us worse than dogs, like the listless skeletons we were becoming. Everyone was exposed to beatings and witnessed death daily. You soon felt no compassion for the victims, so long as it was not you. You told yourself they were lucky to be out of their suffering. This was the first step in losing your soul. This is what I am most ashamed of." At this, he wept profusely.

"Father, my dear father, you were at the hands of the most evil regime in history," young Stashew replied. "You cannot blame yourself for the way you reacted. They intended to turn you from a loving, caring human, into a desensitized, heartless number. This is what they designed this awful, evil camp to do."

His father regained a semblance of composure. Through his tears, he continued, ignoring my remarks. "Each barrack had a 'kapo' who was in charge of us. Most were German inmates brought to Auschwitz from German prisons to provide the direct, daily management of our actions. Our kapo was a violent man named Hans. He beat us all unmercifully, because he enjoyed it. It gave him power. If we did not work fast enough in our daily work deployments, we were beaten and kicked by Hans."

"I noticed that Hans would spend time with the SS officer from my truck. The man that killed my good friend, Tadeusz, under the park willow, was often calling on Hans. I came to learn that his name was Keller. Usually, after I saw them talking, Hans would be more lenient on me, and soon I was not beaten any more by Hans. But the verbal abuse continued."

"Then one day after I had been there for several months, I was sick and suffering from a fever. I had worked with the fever for several days. But this morning I could not get out of my wooden 'bed' to answer roll call. I could not go out on the work detail to construct the additional barracks that were being built."

"After everyone had gone to the roll call, Hans came and began dragging me out of the barracks. I was too lifeless to either resist him or follow his instructions."

"'You Polish dog,' Hans kept repeating in German. 'You'll get me shot. Get on your feet, you swine.'

"Then he began punching me, first in the chest and head, and then exhausted, he stood upright and began kicking me in the stomach with all his might, cursing in German the whole time. I was near passing out from the pain, when I heard the clipped, sterile voice of Keller."

"'What is going on here?', he demanded."

"'This Pole refuses to work, to stand in roll call,' answered Hans, between heavy breaths from the exertion of the beating he gave me.

"'Drag him to the courtyard,' ordered Keller."

"So, Hans began to drag me to the open area where roll call was taken each morning. I was at this point delirious, but even in that state, I could hear Keller yelling at Hans. 'Not here, you idiot – I said take him to the courtyard, by Barrack 11.'

"It was well known throughout the camp that Barrack 11 was the barrack of torture and death. This is where the Germans had specialized cells. Standing cells on the upper floors where the Germans would squeeze four prisoners with only enough room to stand upright. For days, they would be left there as a punishment. Or in the basement of Barrack 11 were specially constructed cells for starving prisoners to death, or sealed cells for suffocating prisoners to death."

"Adjoining Barrack 11 was the courtyard of death, where Soviet war prisoners, Jews, Poles and Roma gypsies were dragged to be shot. Hans was now dragging me to the courtyard of death. Soon, I was to be released from my pain. So I remember thinking, before I stopped thinking altogether."

"I had passed out, but Keller had Hans revive me with water poured on me. I was laying at the base of the wall opposite the entrance to the courtyard. This is the wall where so many were shot dead. I had witnessed this myself. The SS wanted the prisoners to see this brutality, to further instill in us that the rules of humanity did not apply here. Not in this regime, not in this camp, and certainly not here in this courtyard."

"I saw Keller pull his Luger from its holster. He stood in front of Hans and I, the wall to our back. I watched as he released the safety with his thumb. He told Hans to step back a step, which he did. I looked up at Hans to see a sickly familiar smile cross his face. This was the smile he always wore after beating the prisoners. The blood now clotting in my eyes made this snicker all the more sinister. I could not bring myself to look at Keller, so I kept my eye on Hans. I started to fade, and imagined his snicker distort into the face of fear itself."

"The shot rang out, its echo thundered through the heavy second that followed. The fever and the beating distorted my thinking such that I could not register that I had not been shot. It was not until Hans' face distorted into shock, and he fell to the ground that I realized I was still alive. He collapsed rather than fell, his legs buckling under the weight of his being. Hans now lay at my feet. His blood pooling from a wound in his back I could not see. But I could hear Keller standing over him, saying in German what I knew were the same words he said before shooting Tadeusz."

'He who wrestles with monsters must take care…'

"Two shots rang out into Hans' forehead. The first piercing through cleanly, the second sending a large chunk of bone and brain flying through the courtyard. Hans was gone. I now awaited my punishment.

"Keller lowered himself by the waist. It was important that he not be seen kneeling, even on one knee, in front of me.

"'He is dead because he disobeyed my orders. I did not do this for you. You I can kill anytime I desire, just like your friend under the willow tree. Now let me know you can hear me, you bloody, lifeless swine.'

"I was in a near coma, but found the energy to complete his quote. *'…lest he thereby become a monster himself.'* I breathed out in a whisper in German. *'And if you gaze for long into an abyss, the abyss gazes also into you.'*

"Keller's face broadened into a tight, firm smile over me. 'Excellent, you know your Nietzsche.' Keller spun on his heels, holstering his Luger as he walked out of the courtyard, leaving others to attend to Hans' breathless - and my soulless - body."

Chapter Nine

FOUR AM CAME quickly, far too quickly for Stanley. He washed his face with the coldest water the faucet could muster, all the while struggling to assure himself he had the emergency protocol correct that he once had ingrained into every fiber of his being.

He looked in the mirror at his gray, thin beard. It looked ragged, making him appear lifeless and old. Stanley would trim it neatly after the call to assure it did not reveal him for what he was.

He dialed an international number in Prague. The recording in Czech instructed that the number was out of service and no longer monitored. This is what the message had said for the last twenty years, since Stanley and Jean Paul arranged it. After the recording ceased, Stanley keyed in his hotel number followed by his room number. He hung up and called down to the front desk. Stanley knew it would be immediately responded to.

"Yes, Mr. Wisniewski," said the clerk on duty.

"Good morning. I just put a call in to a number in Europe and am expecting a return call in the next hour. Please be sure it gets routed to my room."

Stanley unlocked his briefcase to refresh his memory of the files while he waited to see if his emergency contact would be answered. The answer came quickly, as the morning had. It was 4:37 AM when the phone in the room rang briskly.

Stanley answered, knowing the exchange had to be letter perfect or the phone would go dead immediately.

"Jean Paul?" Stanley asked in a firm voice, quickly continuing with "*Je suis un connaisseur des nocturnes de Chopin.*"

The reply came in French as well, "Yes, but of course, of those who are cultured, who is not?" Not only was the axiom correct to the letter, but Stanley recognized the tone of the voice, despite having not heard it in many years.

Stanley had now switched to Polish, knowing the real Jean Paul would have no trouble following. "I have some work, a very light piece, that I need some help with. Are you still playing these days?"

"*Tak*, of course." Stanley sensed Jean Paul was being very cautious after having not heard from him for so long—other than the encrypted email message from Stanley two nights before.

Jean Paul added, "I am on point." He was in Amsterdam, as requested.

"I need to send you the particular piece of music. Do you have an account I can forward it to? This piece should not be very difficult, but if the piece is played well, it will pay very handsomely."

"Handsomely, *Dobrze.*" Jean Paul appreciated that this code word was also worked into the conversation, confirming that this was indeed Stanley on the line. "Please send the file to the following internet account." Stanley copied down the account web address.

"*Pan* Chopin, what key do you wish me to record this in?"

"C minor. You remember the other pieces we recorded in C minor? If you have any trouble with it, call and leave a brief message for me at the hotel front desk. Reference the Chopin piece and I will contact you again as I just did. I do have a very quick turnaround required on this piece, so please give it your utmost and immediate attention." By protocol Jean Paul would know all responses were to come to the e-mail address from which Stanley sent the file. Any hotel message containing the word Chopin was a code for contact by the back-up contact protocol with extreme caution.

Stanley felt the adrenaline course through his brittle veins, a surge he had not felt for several years. It had the effect of returning youth to him, if only for a few minutes. He felt useful. He felt alive.

Stanley was quickly typing the address name into his email with the encrypted file attached. He had prepared the file to be ready to send as soon as he received the e-mail address. Jean Paul already had the encryption key – the C minor reference – that he would use to make this legible upon receiving. Now that Stanley was sure he was in Amsterdam, he would send the more detailed instructions for Jean Paul to investigate. Stanley hit send.

Later that morning, Stanley, tired but not exhausted, met Lou Cerilla in the hotel lobby to share a ride to the plant. He was pleased that it was to be only the two of them, affording Stanley a little time to dive deeper into his past experiences with Langston Powell.

Stanley began their conversation, picking up on last night's dinner discussions. "So, Lou, I found it interesting that none of your com-patriots at dinner last night share your concerns over Mr. Powell. Seemed like they were trying to get you to rein in your concerns. Am

I reading that right?"

"They're just scared off their asses. He can be vengeful. I'll tell you something about Lanny," said Lou, rising to the bait. "That man is compulsive when it comes to being right. He has to be the smartest person in the room, no matter what. You can see his brain searching for a way out when he's wrong and begins to realize it. Then he will attack the person who was right until he can claim he didn't have all the data, or the person misrepresented something. It is amazing to watch. It's pathological. He loves to argue a point, and will never concede it to somebody other than himself. I guess it works for him, look where he is, and where he is going..."

"Where exactly is he going?" Stanley prompted. "He has only been in this job a couple years."

"Man, that's an eternity for a rising executive. Hell, Lanny claims credit for so many things he didn't actually do, that he can easily claim 'been there, done that' after running Aerospace for two years. Believe me, Lanny's sights are perpetually set higher, and I know he is gotta be trying to set himself up at Corporate for when Roberts retires. Lanny was thinking about that the first week after he was named Aerospace President, I guarantee it."

"Isn't it better to be a top dog at Aerospace, rather than an also-ran in Corporate?" asked Stanley.

"Lanny will gladly take a half step back if it aligns him better to ultimately get Roberts' job. Lanny's only 52, so if he is successful he would have a good ten years at the top of the corporation. Do you realize how much power that is to Lanny, not to mention the dollars that go with it? But I don't think that Lanny was ever driven by the money alone." Cerilla's face was visibly tightening as he spoke.

"He is all about being in control, having others bend to his directions. He is all about strength and power. Once he has it, he is quick to purge those who he feels aren't in his camp. We have seen plenty of that along the way. If he gets to the top spot, a lot of us will retire just to keep from feeling the blunt of his wrath."

"Could he even do Roberts job as CEO?" Stanley was now attempting to keep Cerilla going.

"The guy is Grade A-prime Executive red meat. He is well polished, personable when he wants to be, visionary, strategic and ruthless. He will do whatever it takes to beat out a competitor. And I do mean whatever. Why are you so interested in Lanny, anyway?"

Stanley had felt that Lou was freewheeling, but was now concerned that he had forced the conversation to the subject of Langston Powell one too many times.

"Well, for one thing, he has asked me to join him on a business trip to Poland as an interpreter. I would like to know what kind of a man he is if I am going to invest that much time with him. You know, you learn much about people when you travel with them, I would like to learn this ahead of time if possible. I know you find this hard to believe, but in my first session with him I found him to be very professional and interesting. Even somewhat charming." Stanley was laying it on for a reaction.

Lou's face now sagged with concern as he responded, "Be careful who you travel with. That bastard will charm you until he is done getting what he wants from you. Then he'll drop kick your ass. I'd tell you to ask Ted Barber, but that ain't going to happen, now is it?"

Stanley thought to himself of the file that was sent to Jean Paul. An electronic clipping from the Times of London on Ted Barber's death, with an encrypted file attached. Once decrypted it would be plainly legible and also have Stanley's notation. "My patrons are extremely interested in what really occurred here. Note female accompanist not mentioned. Need story on both. Take necessary funds from the *Jar of Clay*, they will be refunded handsomely within three days."

Protocol said that Jean Paul would respond within 24 hours with an expected value for the "piece" as well as a confirmation date. The *Jar of Clay* reference told Jean Paul this would be expected not to exceed $50K (US). If a response from Jean Paul mentioned the words "Copper Kettle", then that meant the fee would exceed the $50K value. Stanley could then accept the value up to $100K by repeating the phrase "Copper Kettle" in his response. Otherwise, he would give the kill phrase "Malta" in his response, and the operation would be stood down. Now Stanley had but to wait.

Soon Stanley would know what he was dealing with in Mr. Powell. Stanley's gut was telling him to listen to Cerilla and tread cautiously.

Chapter Ten

STASHEW HEARD THE voice of his father continue.

"I woke up days later in the infirmary. At Auschwitz, this was a bad place to be, for if you couldn't work, you weren't any use to the SS. The infirmary didn't waste any real effort on prisoners. Easier to let them die, and replace them. So I was amazed to find I had been there for eight days, in and out of consciousness. I overheard the attendants telling each other that Keller had been inquiring to my status. My heart sank."

"Within a week I had regained enough strength to be returned to my barracks. It was now August 1941 and the weather was beginning to turn in this Polish countryside. The night's cold permeated through the barrack walls to complete the sheer hopelessness of our existence. We knew the bitter cold that awaited us when the fall became winter, and she took her fury on us."

"Roll call at 4:30 AM. Black water coffee. March to work while the camp prison band played grotesquely upbeat music. Return at night for roll call, watered soup and crusts of bread. Beatings. Indiscriminate shootings. Rampant disease. It claimed so many more of the older prisoners, while the younger ones had a chance at fighting it off."

"We had a new kapo, a Bavarian named Metz. He was as brutal as Hans. But not with me. He wouldn't even look at me; he just totally avoided me. Clearly Metz had heard of Hans' fate before Keller."

"Then one day, as I fell in for the morning work detail, Metz told me I was not to go to labor detail any more. I was to report to Barrack 11 and report to Keller. Keller would tell me my new assignment. I was rigid with terror. Any change to our daily miserable existence could only mean more misery and perhaps pain, or death."

"That morning I reported to Keller. He told me I was to do something very important for him. He told me that I was to be placed in the barracks of the Soviet war prisoners. I was to listen to their conversations and report to him. He wanted me to spy on them. I was to report to him daily, but it was urgent that they not know this, he said."

"If anyone was treated worse than us, it was certainly the Jews, and then the Soviet war prisoners. No sooner than the first week I arrived at Auschwitz, I saw these men pulled out of line during roll call and shot by the SS because they were too slow to respond to their number being called. Or they refused to respond in anything other than in a contemptuous tone. This required retribution from the SS, and for the Soviet war prisoners this meant death."

"Of course, the Jews were treated this badly and much worse, but at this point there were not that many there yet. Those that came disappeared, being pulled out of selection and shot straight away, unless they had a critical skill the camp could not do without. But their numbers were constantly increasing. This was a problem for the camp, and little did I realize my new assignment was tied to this."

"I was taken from my barrack and mixed in with the Soviet prisoners to listen to what they spoke of. I was a menial worker among them. For the first several days they said nothing to me or in front of me. Then they slowly began to accept me. They would then talk to each other while I was in the barrack. Of course, we never let them know I spoke Russian. At first I heard only small talk. Soon they were speaking and openly criticizing the Germans and their treatment by the Nazis. Then I would hear discussions about how far the Germans had progressed into Ukraine, and further into Mother Russia itself. Usually the newest POWs brought the latest news in with them. It was all terrible news. No one could stop the Nazis, they seemed destined to take over the world. That was the barrack's talk."

"Also, I heard the stories of the great war crimes being committed by the Nazis in Russia. There was a seething vengeance among the POWs."

"Each day, I was called to meet with Keller in Barrack 11. The Russians were told I was cleaning cells there. They knew these to be the cells of torture and death, and those that spoke some Polish began to ask me of the fate of some of their comrades who had been taken there. Keller was quick to give me information that I was approved to share with the Russians as it made them trust me a little. Soon they were very open with me. After two weeks of listening to the Russian POWs, I began to hear stories of the Germans rounding up the Jews on the Eastern Front, and, after having them dig a mass grave, gunning them down so that they fell in these graves. These stories intensified as more and more POWs came in from the Russian front. The Germans could not be stopped, and their atrocities could not be stood."

"I relayed all of this to Keller. He took very detailed notes as I relayed the information. I almost wondered if the latest news brought in from the most recent Soviet prisoners was information he could not get elsewhere. Or was this simply the organizational ego that the SS needed in order to feel fed. The SS ruled by fear, and certainly these Soviets were greatly afraid of the SS."

"He often asked if there was discussion of experiments, but I had heard nothing of this from the Russians."

"He was interested in what they thought of him, as well. With great fear I told him they called him 'Teuffel Keller' because they thought in German it meant 'Killer Devil.' It was a linguistic abomination, but it stuck. They always referred to Keller as 'Teuffel' or 'Teuffel Keller."

"Then one day in early September, I was awakened and told to report to Barrack 11 after roll call. When I got there, Keller told me to sit in the office where we met until I was called for. I could see out the window onto the main dirt road that was soon abruptly halted by the barbed wire that sectioned the camp. This was the side of Barrack 11 that did not look onto the courtyard of death. The window was open, and I noticed that all the windows were open in the barrack."

"I stared at the macabre sign in front of the barbed wire with the skull and crossbones that read 'halt.' It was not needed. Everyone new not to get near the fence, as the guards were only looking for a reason to shoot a prisoner to break up the monotony of their watch."

"After much time I could hear the ranks of men being shoved downstairs into the basement. Hundreds of them, with many Nazi guards provoking them verbally, their machine guns trained on the crowd, watching for any sign of revolt. But even from the side window I could see the overflow of prisoners and guards corralling them back to the front door of the barracks. I recognized the men wearing the special patches on their prison-striped clothes - Soviet

POWs. I recognized a few as the very men I had recently been barracked with."

"Then there was a short break in time and I heard a second group being crowded in with the first. Once again I could see some of the men through the side window. Now I recognized several of the faces of the other Poles I was quartered with prior to the Hans incident. These men appeared frightened, as anything that broke the awful routine at Auschwitz was frightening in itself. Never was it a good alternative. Life here taught that lesson quickly."

"Once the men were secured in the basement, a guard came for me. I told him that I was instructed to wait there, but he slapped me and told me that Keller had instructed him to take me to a new barrack. I dared not ask why a new barrack was needed. But I soon found out."

"The members of both my old barracks, as well as others, were at this moment in the basement of Barrack 11. The basement had been sealed and this group of men was the first experiment in the use of a German pesticide for disposing of prisoners. That day, 600 Soviet war prisoners and 250 Poles were gassed to death in that basement using Zyklon B, an arsenic based pesticide. At first the dosages dropped into the chamber were too low, and it took an extended period of time for these men to die. But the SS noted this, and increased the amount of Zyklon B until the eventual killing was over in a period of 10-15 minutes."

"This was the experiment that Keller was anxious to see if the Soviet war prisoners knew about. This was the experiment that defined what Auschwitz would become, a true factory of death. From this experiment, the Nazis scaled the pure evil of Birkenau, being built adjacent to the original Auschwitz camp, but so much more deadly in its efficiency of rendering death."

"To this day I cannot help feel that I was partially responsible for the act that led the way to the killing of millions of innocents, that I had helped pave the way."

Stanley saw his father, whose face registered the suffering he was enduring at this telling, explode into a wailing sob that Stanley had never seen from him before. His face contorted in a suffering worse than the ravages of cancer itself, even in these late stages. He feared that his father, who had suffered for all his life, thought that he would suffer for all eternity for the actions he was forced to undertake in the confines and brutality of Auschwitz. He knew his father would embody all the suffering he was forced to witness as an unbearable guilt. Now it released itself in a torrent of emotion that Stanley could not console.

At this point, his mother rushed into the room and quickly draped his face with her wrinkled palms. She spoke to him in Polish, "It is all right, my love. God loves you and forgives you, and soon this will all be over."

His father's body began to shake involuntarily. Stanley thought this was to be the very end, until his mother looked at him and lovingly nodded to the door. She had been through this before. Many times, he thought.

"It will soon be over," she whispered tenderly, repeatedly into his ear.

Stanley left for a walk along the river, but could not clear his mind. This vision of his father's grief haunted his quiet moments from that day to this one.

Chapter 11

STANLEY HAD LABORED through the day, adding comments periodically in the INAR review, but found himself weary after his early morning communications with Jean Paul. He thought as the day wound down about what Jean Paul would be putting in play. Drawing funds from the long dormant Jar of Clay account to cover his expenses would be his first action. Then, he would develop his contacts at the hotel and among the police investigators. They would resist at first, but would give in to the money that Jean Paul had at his disposal for information.

Jean Paul was sure to be aware of the haste required for this type of request. Stanley had caught him early enough to allow him to get to Amsterdam from Paris by the time they connected this morning. The beautiful aspect of it was that the Marquis Continental hotel where Ted Barber was staying when he drowned was but a short walk from the Amsterdam train station. Stanley remembered it well from his operational days in Europe. In fact, in the days of the Soviet Union, when Stanley ran his ring behind the Iron Curtain from Warsaw, Amsterdam was a favorite rendezvous for meeting his superiors face to face, when that was necessary. Jean Paul was with him often, and knew Amsterdam well. Brussels, Oslo, Copenhagen and Paris were also frequent debriefing locations as well. But Amsterdam was a perfect cover. With all the vices that one could pay for there – drugs, sex, liquor – it only seemed natural that westerners in Poland would visit frequently on R&R visits.

Stanley's day was in its late afternoon, when another request came from Langston Powell's office for him to stop by at 5:30 PM. Surely Langston would want Stanley's decision on whether he would join him on the trip to Europe. Stanley had already decided. He walked across the production line again, noticing perhaps for the first time the drones nose to tail glimmering under the halogen lights. Each was somewhat more complete than the one before it, until his walk brought him up to the Fuselage Mate facility, where the wings were joined to the fuselage structures. It was here that he turned left for the shuttle aircraft.

As he walked to the shuttle aircraft, Stanley thought of the havoc these Daedalus Destroyer drones had reaped throughout the world. Having the deadly combination of stealth and precision-guided weapons aloft meant no terrorist was safe at any time. If he could be located, he could be killed.

But Stanley knew from his days at the agency that this also extended to civilians. There were mistakes, of course, where a cluster of burka-wearing women were targeted, thinking these would be terrorists in disguise. The factions that were targeted were quick to show the world their slaughtered remains, where enough was remaining to prove their innocence. Today's was the war of propaganda not unlike what his father witnessed during his war.

Stanley wondered about the inadvertent missile launches Cerilla kept referring to. Were there actual missile firings due to errors in the software?

Stanley knew enough to know that the way these drones worked was that they were constantly seeking targets, so that the target was immediately ready when the order to fire was sent. Is it inconceivable that a drone, in an internal software error, would launch a round by itself, uncommanded? That would explain why if it did the round would not just fall harmlessly to earth. Could this be why the Air Force was so hesitant with the armed drone technology? Could this be a defect that the CIA itself felt it could live with in order to expediently get these assets in the air over Afghanistan, Yemen, Somalia and other key locations? After all, it did not happen very often, the agency would justify.

Stanley could not help but think of the luck of Langston Powell. First, in surviving the faulty software he authored in the missile himself, apparently, by blaming it on Cerilla and others. Then, on the brink of the Air Force walking away from the Daedalus Destroyer program, he succeeds in having it sold in large numbers to the CIA after the terror of the 9/11 attacks on America. The profit margin made Powell the savior of the Aerospace Division, leading to his eventually becoming president of it.

Was it also luck that as he was being considered for the next big promotion to be named effectively CEO in waiting, the one man who likely had the most dirt on him mysteriously drowns in the canals of Amsterdam?

After a calmer passing over the mountains into Irvine, he was now walking through Heritage Hall, literally walking along the timeline history of the Aerospace Business Unit. Slickly produced glossy-mounted images and punctuated text traveled through time to the awarding of various key programs, all the way back to the founding fathers of the firm during the advent of aviation. If only the pioneers of flight had lived to see the talons of death adding to their fledgling wings.

Stanley found it ironic that his jaunt took him from nearly completed aircraft to its component pieces, and from present day back to the founding of the firm. He felt himself walking back in time, from his retirement and the repetition of its days, back to his operational youth where the excitement of uncertainty kept him stimulated nearly continuously.

When he emerged from Heritage Hall into the main hallway of the administrative building, it was a short walk to Langston Powell's outer office.

The President's receptionist said as he walked up to her desk, "Mr. Wisniewski, Mr. Powell is ready to see you, go right in."

Langston was seated behind his desk, surprisingly still on the phone. He extended his open palm over to the round conference table in his office. Stanley took a seat, and wanting to pay attention to something other than the call he would be listening in on, he looked at the many trophies hanging on the walls and under the lights of the cherry bookcase. Among the many pictures of Langston was one with the Secretary of Defense, as well as one with the three-star General who had attended the first production Daedalus Destroyer Drone aircraft acceptance ceremony. These were next to awards for Executive of the Year for the AIAA, and the one he must have been proudest of, under the glass and lights of the bookcase, the Collier Trophy awarded to the program while it had been under his tenure. It was a display that would make Narcissus smile.

"OK, Howard, no problem. I'll have my team run and send those numbers up to your guys tonight. I think once they see them, the decision will be easy. Hey, I need to go, your protégé, Mr. *Vish-nev-ski*, just walked in."

Stanley smiled tightly and looked into Powell's eyes. Langston was smiling broadly and made an open, palm-up gesture with his free hand, as if to say what a coincidence.

It was clear Langston Powell was talking to Howard Burnett, the Executive Vice President and financial controller at corporate head-quarters – the very cover that was provided for Stanley. Would he pregnantly pause at Langston's mention of him, or worse, forget completely and give away the cover? Surely, this was no coincidence, it was Langston testing Stanley, or at least setting him on the defensive.

After a very brief pause, Stanley could hear Langston say into the receiver, "Yes, Stanley, of course. Should I put him on the speakerphone? No, you've got to get to a late dinner. Yes, of course it is already 8:30 there. I completely understand. Good night, and I look forward to your decision on the other matter in the next few days. Thanks, Howard."

The phone handset was lowered back into the cradle of the phone.

Stanley tried not to look relieved.

"Stanley, good to see you again," said Langston, standing and walking from behind the nearly pristine desk to the conference table. He wore no jacket, looking very fit in his suit pants, striped blue and tan tie and pinpoint white shirt. His sleeves were rolled up past his wrists, with only his Patek Philippe watch on his right wrist and his gold Global Defense Analytics thirty-year anniversary bracelet on his left. He continued to smile broadly.

Stanley felt the anticipation of another verbal joust with Langston about to begin.

"So, before you came in I spoke to Howard about your joining me on the trip to Poznan. He said that was no problem, so long as it was good for you. One funny thing, he didn't realize you spoke Polish so effortlessly, he seemed a little surprised as to why I wanted to take you along."

Powell was now seated next to Stanley, and staring straight into his eyes. Stanley felt that Langston was probing, looking for a reaction.

"Well, that's really something that doesn't come up in conversation very readily," Stanley dismissed, half laughing.

"But Stanley, you are so proud of being Polish. Anyone else would have given up the Polish pronunciation long ago. Everybody knows the name as *Wis-new-ski*. There must be half a dozen professional football players with that name over the years. But hanging onto *vis-nev-ski*, now that's pride," said the man who was surrounded by his own smiling face and trophied career.

Powell continued. "But that's OK, Stanley, I want to take advantage of your Polish pride. So are you going to Poznan with me? I could really use you in the meeting with the Polish Government and Air Force." Powell was smiling again. "You know I am not going to take 'no' for an answer."

Stanley had thought through this overnight. If he said no, Langston would hammer hard on Burnett until he did. There was no telling how well Burnett was briefed on this, and if he slipped up, it could blow everything. But what Stanley couldn't tell was how much Powell already knew. This clearly could be a play to get Stanley out of the way until the Board Meeting in which Langston was to be put forth as the new CEO-in-waiting. But Stanley felt he could be more effective in determining if Powell was in any way involved by being in close quarters with him.

Stanley could not help but think this was a rare opportunity. To repent the losses in his life, to right the many wrongs, he must seize it.

"Of course, I'll join you," Stanley said, looking intently back at Powell. "I would love to get to know you better as we travel. And, of course, I would love to show you my home country."

Langston Powell looked over the reading glasses he wore low on his nose to add a semblance of dignity to his otherwise youthful face. "I thought America was your home country?"

"Poland is the country of my culture. The culture I respect and love," clarified Stanley.

"Of course, I would love to show you Warsaw."

"Oh, I bet you would, Stanley. I bet you really would. You know what – I like you, Stanley. You are my kind of guy. We will get along swimmingly." Langston smirked and half winked at him. It seemed to say, "I just got my way – I won."

"We will be leaving Sunday afternoon from here in Irvine and will be traveling on one of the executive jets. Have you ever flown on a company jet, Stanley?" asked Powell through another half-wink.

"No, I have not had that pleasure," Stanley lied to Powell.

"We will be staying in London for one night. I have a meeting with the International Office there on Monday, so I'll clean up on the plane and go directly there. I won't need your services there. I can understand them, even if a few do have the local accent." Langston was laughing smugly now. "You'll be free to take in the sights or whatever."

"Or whatever," echoed Stanley. "I love London. I love to take long walks there. I'll be fine."

Powell ignored him. "Tuesday we'll fly to Poznan, meet with the Poles on Wednesday and Thursday, and then fly onto Warsaw. Friday you can give me that tour you promised me. Then, we will return home. Sound good?"

"Absolutely. What background material do I need?" asked Stanley.

"Don't worry, Stanley," Langston was on his feet again. "We'll cover that on the Gulfstream. Plenty of time to get through that material on the way to London."

Stanley worked his way to his feet. "Then it's settled. I will get the information for the flight from your admin?"

"Don't worry yourself. I'll send a car to the hotel to pick you up. It's the least I can do for an international travel companion, now, isn't it?"

Stanley was committed now. He knew he could finish his report from London if necessary, but if Jean Paul found what he thought he would find, it would be done before they departed on Sunday.

Stanley smiled. "Goodnight, Mr. Powell."

"Langston," he said looking at a file on his desk. "I told you once before, call me Langston."

Chapter 12

THE HUSKY VOICE of Stashew's father called to him. "Stashew, come here, I have more to tell you."

"My son, I remember being in Auschwitz after the gassing experiment incident. I was moved to another barrack. It was winter now, and there was no heat. There was also no food, no rest, and no reason to believe in any future. The cold penetrated you, its bite reminding you of what was left of life – only the ability to feel pain. Death was all around you. Since the day I arrived, people died daily from being worked to death, and now they were freezing to death, too. All the while the Nazi SS perfected their craft. By now they moved out of Barrack 11 and set up a crematorium closer to the gate of Auschwitz. The gassings were being performed on a nearly daily basis.

"I grew weaker and weaker as the months went on. There was just one thing that kept me going. On the parade ground outside our barrack was a large willow tree. It was the only constant in my life for the next few years – other than death and Keller. This willow was the same as the tree that Keller killed Tadeusz Pniewski under. Gracefully bowing away from me always, as if not wishing to witness my fate. But that tree kept me alive. It was the only thing I attached any interest in. I kept wondering, that tree has no function, why are the SS allowing it to stand? Yet it survives, it thrives here in eternal beauty among the grotesque scene of this deadly encampment. That willow intrigued me, consumed my interest, long after I had lost interest in everything else. Seeing that tree every day was all I lived for."

"The winter faded and the promise of spring betrayed us. By now it was clear that the camp we were in had been outgrown by the masses of Jews the Nazis were shipping in from all over Europe. The camp was being enlarged, and, in fact, a new, larger, more efficient camp was being constructed adjacent to ours. Officially named Auschwitz II, it was quickly to become known as Birkenau. It was massively larger and industrially scaled for its sinister purpose."

"Keller continued to look after me. He was saving me for something, but I knew not what. Occasionally, he would put me in with new Russian POWs that came in, but these were fewer and fewer in number. Keller was very anxious to hear what they discussed among themselves. It was clear from the news of the arriving Russians that by the summer of 1943 there had been a major shift. While the Germans had pushed all the way to Moscow, Leningrad and Stalingrad in the previous twelve months, they were now being driven back across the vast Russian steppes. The Russians spoke excitedly of the dead Germans they had encountered on the way back from Stalingrad. The small groups of Soviet POW that were finding their way into Auschwitz were mostly advance scout units that were pushing too far ahead and were captured by the Wehrmacht. The German Army would turn them over to the SS, and those that weren't killed ended up in Auschwitz. I was sent in to spy on them and relay the information back to Keller."

"It brought me great pleasure to see his face tighten when he heard through my German the devastating losses the Wehrmacht were taking at the hands of the Russians. When I named the cities and towns these POWs had marched through before being captured, it was easy to see Keller's face distort as he plotted the advance on the unfurled map between us. He could see the Red Army was heading directly toward Warsaw in the north, Krakow in the south, and Auschwitz/Birkenau. I could see his worry tighten his face as he worked through his calculations realizing how fearfully soon it could arrive."

"The Russian POWs were never kept long. They were starved and interrogated before they were killed, and I was always placed with them until then, to listen in on their discussions."

"But as the summer of 1943 turned to fall, they began to dwindle in numbers. Keller's thought this was a bad omen; it showed in his face. Certainly, the news from the front that Keller was hearing was not comforting. The Russians continued to drive the Germans back to the West. But the trains filled with innocent Jews taken from all over Europe continued to pour into Auschwitz and Birkenau. The smell of death was everywhere."

"One morning, standing in roll call in the winter's frost in early 1944, shivering, I looked past the guards at that mournful willow. For some reason, I don't know where it came from, my head I am sure, I alone heard the sadness of Chopin's Nocturne Opus 6, note for delicate, tearful note. Yet within its sadness, I could hear subdued notes of hopefulness. I scanned the faces of the German guards, wondering how tormented in death they would look when the Red Army arrived. For if there was one thing I was sure to relay in great detail to Keller, and I am sure he spread it to the other guards, were the details of the atrocities the Russians were committing on the Germans they overran. They were merely paying back the Germans for the inhumane cruelty inflicted on the Russian people before the tide had turned. I could see their faces, my captors, distorted with the fear and terror that they themselves had delighted in seeing on the faces of the dying here in Auschwitz. I took personal delight in this morbid vision of my German captors."

Stanley's father's face was hollow with the stress of relaying all these details. His eyes vacant as the soul he described in Auschwitz. Only then it did it strike Stanley how long this man had suppressed all this. He was the first and only person to whom he had ever spoken these words. He was racing with death to complete his story.

He continued, after a brief rest of several breaths. "My world was nearly over, but I did not fear death, for no longer did I think I could resist. Then Nietzsche - the very philosopher the Nazis built their warped, evil foundation upon – Nietzsche's words came to me as a distorted solace:

"*He who fights with monsters must take care, lest he thereby become a monster himself.*"

"*And if you gaze for long into an abyss, the abyss gazes also into you.*"

Chapter 13

STANLEY FOUND HIMSELF back in his room at his hotel in Palmdale, California. He was hunched over his laptop. Now that contact had been made with Jean Paul, he would check each day, soon several times a day for updates. While he did not expect to receive an update this evening – and it was now the middle of the night in Amsterdam – he was surprised to find a file that he had downloaded. He ran it through his encryption key, and was preparing to read the extracted text. It read in Polish:

"Productive first day – contacts in Dutch government confirms drowning as cause of death, but also added additional drug present. Cocaine. Likely contributing factor to accident."

"Contact confirmed young lady found dead in subject's apartment from overdose of same."

"Hotel contact confirms a third woman was present that evening – local prostitute goes by name Annette. Was seen dashing out of hotel lobby just before Barber came out of the lobby in an apparent disoriented state, seemingly exiting hotel to find Annette."

"Barber was seen on bridge over nearby canal standing on railing looking for her, before falling into canal. He was not found until early next

morning by police, wedged under the embankment."

"Annette represents witness to what occurred in the hotel room. Next action is to find her and question her. Will require dipping into Copper Kettle. I understand time is of essence – will act swiftly."

"Also, hotel contact confirms Annette was a regular for these two. Seen here several times before – perhaps five. That is all for now."

Stanley was stunned. So this was why this was such a delicate matter for the firm. The firm knew Barber not only drowned, but he left behind the dead corpse of another London office employee – Cecily Kendall, his office mate. Did the firm even know about the prostitute Annette? Stanley doubted it.

But it explained one thing – why Barber liked frequenting Amsterdam. He had his vices, and his vices were safe, he thought, in the land of vice for profit.

Stanley typed the brief response in Polish. He reread it carefully before encrypting it: *Message from Zachariah – your message received and understood. Copper Kettle is deep, access as needed. Send updates regularly. Plan to meet me in London on Monday afternoon – same location as last engagement there. Also plan to meet me in old town Warsaw next Friday evening between 6 and 9 PM at Rynek Stare Miasto. Do not acknowledge me at this meet. Bring the endowment to Rynek in Warsaw. Urgent that endowment is functional. Details to be shared at London meeting."*

Stanley knew Jean Paul would recognize his operational name Zachariah, as well as the protocol for the meeting in London. Of course, he would know Stanley's reference to the endowment. He would certainly know the definition of "functional".

Stanley encrypted and sent the message. But what bothered him now was what Stanley had seen in Barber's files. He had been suspected of drug use while on the decline on the Daedalus Destroyer program after his marriage failed. He had provided evidence that he could not possibly have been using cocaine – yes, here it was, it was cocaine – because he was extremely allergic to this class of drugs. The case was dismissed. As Stanley eyed the ethics complaint file, one thing was jumping out at him – the case had been reported anonymously – but it was recorded in the ethics brief that the anonymous party was Langston Powell. The same Langston Powell that had dinner with Barber, sans Cecily and Annette, only hours before Barber's death.

Chapter 14

"I WAS AWAKENED one morning, my son, by Keller. He told me to come quickly. That he and I would be taking a trip, and that we were both excused from roll call. It was the spring of 1944, and the dawn light was just revealing the terror of the camp that had been hidden from the world under the weight of darkness's veil."

"I was terrorized by this. I was sure Keller was taking me to kill me. Only then did I realize I had not completely given up on life, because at this unusual request I feared death. My hands trembled as Keller secured me to the back of the German army truck. I had wondered if it was the very same vehicle that was used to bring me to this camp of death against every fiber of will that I had."

"The morning air was brisk, but not the penetrating cold of winter. The truck was open to the outdoors, and I was secured to the fencing of the bed. We drove past the now reviving willow tree and through the gates that bore the lie 'Work will set you free' in German. Soon we were in the morning-lit Polish countryside."

"Keller drove faster as the sun rose higher in the sky. I sensed an anticipation in him that I feared. I could hear him humming some German folk music that I recognized from his window. He was free of the camp, and was relieved to be so."

"We drove into the country for an hour. I began to think that if he only wanted to kill me he would have done so by now. He wanted me for another reason, I would soon find out."

"The countryside of this region, Silesia, was beautiful. It had not been as devastated as the north near Warsaw had been in the Blitzkrieg. It was alluring, my eyes teared as I looked for the first time in over three years on the beauty of the country of my birth."

"Keller saw me wide-eyed in his rear view mirror and yelled out in German, 'So you like this part of Germany, do you? Yes, it is space for us to grow into – living space.' He used the German word '*leben-sraum*,' the word used to describe the Nazi policy of taking by force adjacent territories for the sake of the German nation's peoples. Of course, my Poland was one of the countries defiled in the process."

"He reminded me again that my country had been divided, not only by the Austrians, the Prussians and the Russians so unjustly in the distant past, but it had been shred in half in this war by the Germans and Russians. They greedily fed on their remnants, until the day Hitler betrayed the Russians and invaded them in June of 1941. But now, after the Battle of Stalingrad had ended in early 1943 with a massive Soviet encirclement of the German Sixth Army, it was quite clear that the Russians had driven back the Germans, and by this summer of 1944 would soon be closing in on Warsaw itself."

"The truck turned off the main road on a dirt path to a farm road, nestled among the foothills of the mountains. Keller unexpectedly decelerated, bouncing me about in the bed of the truck until we came upon a farmhouse and barn. The road was very rough even at the reduced speed Keller negotiated. I thought I might be thrown from the truck if not for my bindings. My wrists bled, and I was once again subject to the cruelty of my German master."

"Keller slammed on the brakes as the truck wheeled in the dirt outside the farmhouse. By now, it was the full light of morning and the farm was awake. It was clear Keller had been here before."

"An old man came out of the front door of the farmhouse, fear painted his face. He came down the steps as Keller drew his pistol – the old Luger that the guards carried. The higher-ranking officers had newer pistols, as some of these Lugers dated back to before World War I. I watched carefully as Keller released the safety by pushing the safety release lever forward and upward with his thumb. He shot several rounds into the air for effect. The old man crouched in fear, instinctively raising his hands to his head."

"Keller yelled at me in German, saying, 'My young Polish dog, tell this old Polish dog that we want potatoes and meat.'

"So this was why I was brought, to be an interpreter. I told the old man that Keller wanted potatoes and meat, and that this man was a killer. He had better comply. I was still bound in the back of the truck as the old man replied,

'But another German truck was just here last week. They took everything. I only have enough potatoes to feed my family. I have not had meat for years.'

"At the old man's muttering of this last phrase, it became evident that a young girl of about sixteen was watching this disruption of the farm's day from inside the house. The old man saw me watching her and yelled for her to hide in the house. He feared the Nazis, knowing them for the beasts that they were."

"Keller retorted, 'What is going on? I see no potatoes in my truck. Tell the old man to tell whoever he has in the house to come out here now, or I will go inside and shoot them.'

"I had wondered if Keller actually understood the old man's Polish, but then I realized he had merely seen me watching the girl, and her disappearance into the house as the old man spoke."

"Keller walked directly up to the old man. He stood inches from his face with his Luger in his right hand. In his left hand, he grasped a document."

"Tell him, by order of the Reich, he is to fill my truck with potatoes. This order does not restrict me from shooting him, so advise him to give up his crop or bear my wrath. Also, he is to have the girl and any others come out to witness his death."

"I translated and warned the old farmer that this man enjoyed killing, not to give him a reason to do so."

"The old man reached into his pocket in a quick motion. Keller, surprised by this motion, drew his right hand back and hit the old man across the face as hard as he could, fearing that the man was reaching for a weapon."

"As the back of his hand smashed into the old man's cheek, it still gripped he Luger. The impact of the action caused Keller to involuntarily trigger the pistol, firing only inches away from the man's ear. The old man fell to the ground, clutching his ear. There was no blood. The noise of the discharge of the pistol so close to his ear caused the man to cup his ear. The daughter, who had been watching this from inside the house, feared her father had been shot and lay bleeding, dying in the dirt. She ran from the house screaming, '*Tata! Tata!* Please do not kill my *tata*...'

"The old man lay shaking at the boots of Keller. He yelled to me, still secured to the truck bed above them all. He yelled to me, 'Paper. I have only paper to show him.'

"His voice was stammering with fear, and I was sure the pain in his jaw was throbbing. I relayed this to Keller, who response to me was, 'Tell this dog he nearly lost his life reaching for that. Tell him to pull it out slowly.'

"The man, panting in the dirt, his daughter kneeling by his side, clutching him like a small child, held the paper drawn from his pocket and reached it to Keller to inspect. It was the Reich's order from last week to surrender all his produce to the German Army – the Wehrmacht. Keller recognized it immediately. His face registered that he was faced with returning to camp with nothing, certainly displeasing his superiors."

"Tell him this means nothing. Tell him to find me whatever he can, or I take his beautiful, young daughter back to Auschwitz with me. She will be very popular with all of us there."

"The father of the girl pulled his daughter close to him, understanding the lust that was now in full fire in Keller's eyes."

"Keller reached down, and before I could translate, grabbed the young girl in her peasant dress and yanked her upright against him. His thick arm wrapped around her, his palm flat against her midsection. The old man's eyes lit with a terror that was much greater than the risk of losing his own life. He feared he would lose his only daughter. I translated Keller's threat."

"In response, the father pleaded to me. 'Please, please, don't let him take her. She is all I have. Her *matka* is dead, killed by German soldiers last year. She is my only reason for life itself. Please tell him to spare her.'

"Keller's hands now roamed the curves hidden beneath the daughter's loose, worn dress. His eyes lit with enjoyment at once again having a woman under his touch, even if the woman was but a young girl. I feared for what was coming next."

"I told the old man he needed to provide whatever stores he had hidden from the Germans and quickly if he wanted to see his daughter unharmed. Better they should starve to death than lose her to the desires of this beast. Even as I said this, I knew Keller would take the girl and kill the old peasant also just to fulfill all his grotesque animal needs."

"The father looked at my emaciated body, starving from years at the hands of these monsters, warning him of how serious a situation this was. He realized how dire his position was and got to his feet feebly. He walked to his barn and though it was empty, went to the very back to move some fencing that made a false wall. He cried as he carried the last of his food, four sacks of potatoes and two sacks of beets that he had hidden to keep them both alive.

Keller never offered to free me to assist him, as he was preoccupied. His face was consumed by lust. He had the anticipation of a starved man about to feast."

"As the old man walked past them to make the six trips, Keller, who had now holstered his gun, gasped greedily at the young girl's body. His hands followed along her ribs up to grasp her young breasts."

"Keller raised his left hand to her face, covering her mouth as he slid his right hand down the top of her dress, which he had enjoyed unbuttoning. The girl's face registered shame and fear simultaneously. She could feel the breath of this beast panting heavily on her neck. Keller continued this as the old man loaded the last of his hidden trove of subsistence onto the truck bed, only inches from my feet. The old man watched in agony as his daughter was assaulted as he loaded the truck."

"The old man had finished loading the truck when Keller began raising the dress of the girl, bunching it with his now freed right hand on her hip, his left hand still over her mouth. Keller had intentionally waited for the father to finish, in order to force him to watch the German defile his cherished daughter. Her dress slowly lifted like an uneven theater curtain, revealing her full hips in the morning light."

"At this point, a German service car came rambling up the dusty drive. Keller released the girl in a frustrated motion, the curtain of her humble dress raining down to restore her peasant dignity. Yet her face showed no release of the shame she had experienced at the hands of Keller, who now pushed her into the arms of the old man before the car had drawn near."

"The car pulled up close next to Keller. The two officers in the vehicle demanded to know why he was foraging on their territory. Keller held out his orders, and yelled that he was on assignment to provide his unit food for Auschwitz. Between this, and their seeing that he was not only SS, but also that his collar and sleeve bore the skull and crossbones insignia of the SS *Totenkopf*, they looked at each other in a startled state."

"Keller went on to brag how this old Pole had been hoarding food, and how he was able to wrestle free the food on the truck from the old man. The farmer looked at the two officers, certainly he recognized them. He did not fear them. It dawned on me that these men had been here before, possibly executing last week's orders, and had allowed the old man to keep enough food for himself and the girl. They had arrived just in time."

"The officers pointed to me and asked what was going on with the prisoner."

"Keller snorted 'That prisoner speaks better German than you do, *Oberleutnant*. His Russian is flawless also. That Pole has kept himself alive as my personal interpreter.'

"Then Keller laughed heartily. 'He will be my ticket out of here if the Russians come...'

My father's eyes raised to meet mine. Hollow, sullen, they said, "Now I understood why I was being kept so barely alive. I was his insurance to help him escape the impending Russian onslaught."

Chapter 15

STANLEY HAD CONTACTED Marlow. He had told him he was a few days from having confirmation one way or the other of Powell's involvement in the Barber death. But despite this update he knew he still lacked a motive.

Then he asked for what he was sure he would be denied. He asked for a meeting with the Chief Ethics Officer of the Corporation, Juliana Pierce. Stanley had been through the ethics files provided by Pierce via Marlow, and they were extremely insightful. In one case, Langston Powell had anonymously leveled a drug use charge against Barber, only to find that Barber was highly allergic to that particular drug, cocaine. Barber wandered out of the hotel in a stupor, everyone assuming he was high or drunk, and ended up in the canals of Amsterdam. Jean Paul had already confirmed that the autopsy showed cocaine in his system. Therefore, Powell had a method. But Stanley still did not have a motive. Why did Powell turn so sour on Barber after promoting him so aggressively on the Daedalus Destroyer Program?

Now, Juliana Pierce sat before him in a non-descript office within the SCIF, a Secure Communication Information Facility, that Marlow had arranged for them. This was the forum for classified discussions, as long as the SCIF was cleared for the particular discussion's security level. Marlow had personally contacted Pierce, and told her that their CEO, Everett Roberts, had given the instructions that she was to answer any questions that Mr. Wisniewski might direct to her. He also assumed that when Juliana Pierce asked Stanley's identity, Marlow told her not to.

"Not in your need-to-know, I'm afraid, Juliana. Just rest assured Mr. Wisniewski is a friend of the front office and properly vetted," Stanley could hear Marlow covering his tracks.

Stanley knew there would be passive, or even aggressive resistance, to this executive sharing her delicate secrets, even when directed to do so. It was a response that the intelligence officer in Stanley not only understood, but respected.

"Ms. Pierce, thank you for agreeing to meet with me today," Stanley started.

Juliana Pierce was a southern professional that had risen through the ranks to the corporate headquarters. She was thin, even now in her mid-forties. Her clothing was corporate modern, but with the flair of vintage Chanel. Her hands and wrists were bound by the elegant gleaming strands of diamonds and sapphire – a tennis bracelet dueled with what Stanley took for a two-carat, diamond wedding ring, as well as a sapphire accent ring on the opposite hand. The effect was completed by the delicate frosting of a fresh, French manicure accenting each of the long, immaculate nails of her slender fingers. It was as if her extravagant appearance was carefully balancing the staid, impartial persona her position required. Was she subliminally saying she was not as bland as the position she held? No, there was nothing subliminal going on here, Stanley surmised.

She had been told he was an official investigating the Barber matter, but nothing more specific than that. She believed at this level of Corporate instruction, it was not advisable to ask further questions. Juliana Pierce had gotten to this position by reading the corporate tea leaves, and she deemed herself to be very adept at doing so. Her perception was that this was a high-level government investigation of some sort. It was highly unusual not to have legal in the room, but she was told she would be alone with Stanley and was to answer any questions that were put forth to her regarding the ethics cases of Mr. Barber and Mr. Powell.

Ms. Pierce had access to all ethics cases across the corporation, and very often was the determining officer in any cases that involved the higher levels of the firm's leadership. She could be tough, especially for the Director level. More than one Director's career had either stalled or ended based on ethical complaints made against them by their subordinates.

She wore the aggressive resolution of the Directors' cases like a badge of honor, shining like a beacon bright enough to overpower her bejeweled appearance.

But at the Executive VP and President level, she had been a staunch protector of those who could befriend her career.

She sat before Stanley, nervously adjusting a Wedgwood Jasperware Cameo broach she wore in contrast to her charcoal gray lapel-less suit. She was clearly uncomfortable being in the unusual position of answering questions, instead of asking them herself. Her mind was anxious, as if she were a medieval torturer, strapped to the in-quisitor's table, knowing the expert methods that were about to be applied. Her excellently made-up face wore a concern born of professional respect.

"Mr. *Wiz-new-ski*," she said, with a tight, instantaneous flashing of a smile at the corners of her mouth, possibly denoting her pride on intentionally Anglicizing his name to distract him, "I just want to make one thing clear before we begin. While I have been instructed to assist you by answering any questions you may have, I have objected directly to Mr. Roberts office. As Chief Ethics Officer of this corporation, I am entrusted with details affecting many of our leadership. They entrust their careers and their very ability to act decisively in their positions to the very impartiality and anonymity that my office affords them. So I want you to know, that I have filed a letter of concern to the office of Mr. Marlow, and copied Mr. Everett's office, objecting to this session. While I am instructed to continue, I wanted to make sure *you* were aware of this." The slight southern twang of her speech resonated on the *you*, as if to say she was still partially in control.

"Yes, thank you, Ms. Pierce, I was made aware of that." Stanley decided to lie in response. It would highlight his cryptically elevated stature in her eyes. If she had just lied to him about the objection, then they were on even terms.

Stanley reflected on the woman who sat before him. Was she the power hungry opportunist her file reflected? If so, how much he revealed to her by the questions he asked was crucial. It certainly could get back to Powell, in an attempt to curry favor.

"Actually, I found it interesting that you registered your objection on behalf of your firm's leadership, when most Ethics Officers describe themselves as representing all employees, especially those subject to the very power of the executives you referenced," Stanley started, wiping back the gray, straight locks that had fallen carelessly onto his forehead with his open left palm. "*The strong take advantage of the weak,*" Stanley could hear echo through his silent conscience.

"Now that your grievance has been stated, I hope you will be fully forthcoming in response to my questions."

Juliana Pierce adjusted her impeccable suit jacket down against her shapely waist, as if to disguise the squirming nature of the response to Stanley's insight. "Yes, of course. Let's begin," she responded crisply, again as if she controlled the situation.

Stanley intentionally took a second to delay and allow the tension to build. He scanned the desk before him, resting his eyes on the gray phone in front of him with the reminder card suspended on a clip stand above it that said merely, "Hello." It was a reminder to the answering party in this secure facility to stay as unidentified as possible on the line.

"Exactly how many executives does your firm have, Ms. Pierce?" The questioning began.

"One-thousand, two-hundred and ninety-nine," she responded, this time her tight corner-mouth smile flashed with a perceptible but subtle head nod. Stanley sensed her nervousness. She continued, "1025 Directors, 6 Executive Directors, 225 Vice Presidents, and 43 Higher Level Executives."

She seemed pleased that she had this level of detail. Stanley had hoped she would, it was the essence of easing her guard.

"And what percent of the ethics cases of the Corporation involve these Executives?" Stanley asked.

"Well, actually, very little. You have to understand that that most cases are brought at the co-worker or manager levels. At the Director level and above they are more rare. About 6.5%." She stretched her palms flat against her thighs, which her Chanel suit skirt covered in a tight taper as she sat upright.

"But these cases do happen, do they not? I have been told you can be very tough on these Executives when necessary," Stanley said in a slow, unhurried voice.

"Well, not myself alone. When it becomes necessary, the officers of the corporation act on these cases, Mr. *Wiz-new-ski*." The tight smile flashed again with the snapping head nod to the left.

"But Ms. Pierce, you are modest. Isn't it your office that vets these cases and decides which are severe enough to be taken to the Corporate council of officers?"

"Yes, that is exactly what my responsibilities are," she answered firmly.

"So you have had ethics cases of all types levied at this level of leadership – sexual misconduct, illegal substance abuse, security concerns." Stanley rattled of the list slowly for impact.

"We are no different than any other American, or for that matter, multinational corporation, Mr. *Wiz New Ski*. I am sure all the members of the Forbes 500 have issues they deal with at this level."

"Yes, of course, Ms. Pierce. I am sure you are absolutely correct. I have interest in the person of the recently deceased Mr. Barber. Thank you for providing me his files. It appears Mr. Barber had the entire trifecta covered."

"I am not following your last comment." He had noticed it was the first time she had lowered her guard since they began.

"Forgive me, it is a horse racing term I thought was well known."

"Oh, I see," she said earnestly. "Sorry, but I don't believe in gambling."

You are gambling with your career, right now, Stanley thought but did not say.

"Well, Ms. Pierce, isn't it true that as his marriage was breaking up, Mr. Barber was accused of having an office affair with a somewhat younger co-worker?"

"That matter was extensively investigated," she began, showing confidence that she had been prepared for this line of questions. "Mr. Barber was cleared because the relationship with his fellow employee began after he was legally separated from his wife, and Mr. Barber had no authority over the young lady as she did not work on the Daedalus Destroyer program."

Stanley feinted reading the case file in his hands for effect.

"But the matter was documented in his files. Interestingly, this case file was last updated just before the selection of Mr. Powell's successor as the Daedalus Destroyer Program Manager, a promotion from Deputy Program Manager that Mr. Barber was apparently very qualified for, but did not get. Were you involved in the selection process for that position?"

"Yes, Mr. Wisniewski, I am a standing member on the selection board for all positions at that level and above. I believe you are already aware of that."

"Yes, of course. I just wanted you to confirm that. Please recall that I had asked for complete transparency in my questions to you and I believe you were instructed to provide exactly that. So, my next question to you..." Stanley again paused for effect, "was this brought up in the selection process for the Program Manager selection to replace Mr. Powell?"

"Forgive me, Mr. Wisniewski. I am very uncomfortable with this line of questioning." Juliana shifted her weight, while pulling down at the tight corners of her mouth.

Stanley reached for the phone at the desk that was between them. "Would you prefer I call Mr. Everett's office to reinforce the directions regarding your objections?"

"No. That won't be necessary." She arched up in her chair with the suddenness of a spark shorting across a live circuit.

"So, even though Mr. Barber was cleared, this question was raised in the selection process?" asked Stanley.

"Yes." Suddenly, Ms. Pierce resorted to short factual answers.

"Who raised the Ethics case in this selection process?"

"Mr. Powell."

"Was it typical for the exiting executive to be part of the selection panel?"

"Yes."

"And this case was originally registered anonymously, but in the file notated to be by one Ms. Angela King?"

"Yes."

Stanley looked into the eyes of the woman before him, coaxing, "What was Ms. King's position at the time this case was opened?"

"Ms. King was Mr. Powell's Executive Assistant at that time." Ms. Pierce answered coldly.

"Was that fact discussed in the selection?"

"No. Ethics discussions respect the anonymous nature of these complaints," she responded.

"So Miss Pierce," Stanley reviewed. "You sat at the selection panel and quietly watched as Mr. Powell discussed an ethics case filed anonymously by his assistant while making the case that Mr. Barber was unfit to succeed him as Program Manager for the Daedalus Destroyer Program? Was that ethical conduct in itself?"

Juliana Pierce had now gone from nervous to defiant. "Mr. Wisniewski, I am sharing my experiences with you very openly. I am not on trial here. My responsibilities require a level of subtlety and respect to anonymity that you may not share. But in answer to your question, yes, the name of the individual bringing the claim was not discussed."

"So, I suspected," Stanley drew a long heavy breath. "Was the accusation that had been filed earlier of Mr. Barber's alleged drug use raised?"

"Yes," she answered in a short nervous bark.

"By Mr. Powell?" asked Stanley.

"Yes. But I was quick to point out that Mr. Barber was cleared of both of these allegations."

"But only after Mr. Powell made the point that Mr. Barber was in fact dating another younger employee of the firm? Which, although he was cleared of it, was factual."

"Yes, but…"

Stanley cut her off aggressively. "So the panel now knew Mr. Barber was indiscreet, if not unethical, and when you mentioned that he was cleared of the earlier drug accusation, the damage was already done, wasn't it?"

Juliana Pierce did not answer.

"Wasn't it, Ms. Pierce?" said Stanley, raising and firming his voice accusingly. "Mr. Barber was effectively dismissed as a candidate. He was damaged goods, an executive gone awry, in the eyes of the panel. He was not selected after all."

"Yes, that is effectively what occurred. But Mr. Barber was exhibiting some bizarre behavior for an executive at this level, even if it fell within the realm of ethically acceptable. Due to this, he was not selected."

"His marriage had just crumpled under the strain of his job." Stanley pushed back, sensing her tension. "Was that considered?"

Pierce snapped back forcefully, "Mr. Wisniewski, I knew Ted Barber very well. He was no angel. His penchant for the young female engineers in the firm was well-known, let's say. The panel made the right decision."

"So there were additional cases against him of this sort?" Stanley demanded.

"Well, no. But his reputation proceeded him somewhat."

"At a selection panel of the Corporation's highest ranking executives?" Stanley asked with mock incredulity.

"The character of the executives is a high concern in making these selections. Mr. Barber's reputation caught up with him," Ms. Pierce said calmly.

"With the assistance of Mr. Powell and his Executive Assistant's anonymous ethics complaints. So very interesting." He paused, again watching Ms. Pierce's nervous gymnastics with her skirt.

Stanley pressed her in her nervousness. "Why do you think Mr. Powell was so averse to Mr. Barber taking over the Daedalus Destroyer program?"

"I have no idea – you will have to ask Mr. Powell that," she responded.

"Project Artemis?" asked Stanley, catching her off guard.

Now Ms. Pierce was very concerned. "Mr. Wisniewski – that is a classified project. We will stop this discussion right now." She rose to her feet.

Stanley lifted the phone. He spoke softly in to the handset. "Can you come in now, please?"

He turned to Ms. Pierce. "That is exactly why I requested this discussion be held in this classified office space."

The door opened and in walked the senior security officer for the site. Ms. Pierce recognized him immediately. He turned to her and said non-expressively, "Juliana, good to see you again. I have been asked to inform you that as of this morning, Mr. Wisniewski was read into Project Artemis. Also, you are already acknowledged on the project and this space is cleared for Project Artemis discussions. The phone is an unclassified line, and as such I need to remove it before your classified discussion commences. We have access to a crypto-key secure phone in this area, but I am advised you will not need that this afternoon. I will leave the room, but understand you are cleared for Project Artemis discussions to proceed." With this, the security officer exited the room, phone set in hand, closing the door behind him.

Juliana Pierce looked nervously at Stanley. She sat back in her chair, knowing she had been outplayed. The light wrinkles about her eyes were now heavy with definition.

"So, now it is clear why you wanted to have this session in this SCIF area. I thought it was just to keep away from prying eyes, but you fully intended to discuss Project Artemis all along," she said.

On her face, Stanley could see the full understanding of the corner that he had painted her into.

"Yes, so it would seem," Stanley said softly with a wry smile. "Shall we continue?"

"The third leg of the trifecta – we've discussed the sex and drugs, so let's talk about the classified nature of what's behind all this. Ted Barber had filed an ethics complaint of his own against Langston Powell a year or so after Powell was named the Daedalus Destroyer Program Manager. The ethics file only said that the nature of the complaint dealt with classified materials pursuant to Project Artemis." At this, Stanley arched an eyebrow, looking up from the materials he read from.

Stanley looked at her accusingly, but stayed silent before continuing to let the tension build.

"Now I know from being read into the project this morning, that Artemis is related to the launch system of an advanced missile system that was designed to be launched from the Daedalus Destroyer Drone. I also understand that the strike weapon's main guidance algorithm was developed by Langston Powell's team before he became Daedalus Destroyer Program Manager. Now, Ms. Pierce, what was the nature of the complaint filed by Mr. Barber, who was the Daedalus Destroyer Chief Engineer?"

"That it didn't work." Ms. Pierce had returned to the clipped factual answers.

"Isn't it unusual for a Program's Chief Engineer to bring an ethics complaint against the Program Manager for a classified technical issue? What exactly didn't work? Yes, here it is." Stanley shuffled the classified report in front of him. "Unauthorized launches – one during test and development, and two more operationally, in Yemen while under CIA control. Very nasty. The most recent took out a village gathering celebrating something or other. 13 dead. Very nasty repercussions, indeed, had the CIA not covered it up."

Perspiration was now visible on the brow of Ms. Pierce.

"Mr. Barber had discussed the issue with Mr. Powell. Mr. Powell argued that the problem was on the aircraft side of the interface. Mr. Barber felt he had proved it was not. Mr. Powell had directed Mr. Barber to make sure the issue was fixed under Project Artemis."

Pierce continued, "Mr. Barber felt this was not within the allowed tasking of the project. Mr. Barber further asserted that the test results from Mr. Powell's previous team must have been falsified, because the performance observed in testing was significantly less than that reported in Mr. Powell's previous classified project summary."

She breathed a heavy breath, having now unloaded all that she had hoped to conceal coming into this session.

Stanley wanted to tie the factual threads together. He began, "So if I am understanding this sequence of events correctly, Mr. Powell runs a team developing a critical weapon to be launched from the world's most advanced tactical drone. It earns him the visibility to be considered for the Program Manager of that very drone program, one of the prime executive positions in the firm. The only problem is that the chief engineer of the program discovers that the prize weapon doesn't work as it should once testing starts, and performs even worse in the field. After discussions with the program manager, he convinces himself that his new program manager had falsified the capabilities of the weapon that made him corporately famous in the first place. He files a rare, classified ethics complaint. The program manager is protected because so few people are cleared to the project, and he is able to clear himself mainly because the problem is so technically complex. But the chief engineer continues to press the issue, perhaps threatens to become a government whistle blower. Next thing we know, the chief engineer is facing allegations of drug use and then sexual misconduct, both of which he is cleared of, but that effectively ruin his reputation. He is reassigned to International, and most conveniently, is read off Project Artemis. He no longer has the access needed to continue with his complaint. He is shipped overseas to London, conveniently out of the way. Is that right, Ms. Pierce?"

Juliana's face said what she did not want to. She was amazed that Stanley had gotten this deep into this complex web of intrigue so quickly.

"Yes. Something along those lines, yes." She was now fully unburdened, her nervousness replaced with a feeling of empty dread.

"But I left out the rest of the story. The program manager, his secret now safe, goes on to be promoted to President," In his mind, he also thought, *and now is under consideration for the office that will ultimately make him CEO of the entire firm.*

Stanley continued aloud. "Thank you, Ms. Pierce, you have truly provided me the insights I needed. I don't need to remind you that this discussion is classified and not to be discussed with anyone outside this room. I assume you realize that means anyone other than myself. You are neither to discuss it with Marlow, nor Mr. Powell."

"Yes, of course," she said in as dismissive a note as she could affect.

"I have a couple of final questions, Ms. Pierce." He paused for effect. "What was the disposition of Mr. Powell in this case?"

"You have the file right in front of you," Juliana retorted.

"Are you refusing to answer my question?" Stanley asked, arching his gray eyebrow.

Juliana Pierce audibly hissed, "Mr. Powell was found to be fully in the clear."

"Was the technical defect corrected after Mr. Barber was read out of the program?"

"Yes."

"You were later promoted from Director to Executive Director of Ethics, by Mr. Powell himself, after he became President?"

"Yes, but if you are insinuating..."

"I insinuate nothing, Ms. Pierce, I only point out how tidy this all appears once all the facts are available for review." Ms. Pierce began to object when Stanley cut her off with a simple, "Thank you, Ms. Pierce, we are through and you may leave."

Juliana Pierce stood sharply, looked hard at Stanley, and turned and left the classified SCIF. Stanley was sure as she left that there was, despite his warnings, a chance this interview might be retold in detail to Langston Powell.

Stanley thought, *I now have the motive for Mr. Powell permanently removing Mr. Barber. No need to have anyone around to object to his being named to his next and most powerful position.*

He further surmised, *it makes no difference if she shares the details with Powell, as we are past the point where that matters.*

Chapter 16

"STASHEW, MY SON, death was all around me. Every time I craved its release from the suffering I was enduring, the will to live would swell up inside me, just enough to overcome my madness," his father continued.

"It was the summer of 1944. The death machine that was Birkenau had now been in full gear for some time. It consumed innocent life and spewed its ungodly ash, falling like a plague of the dead upon the living. Daily it reminded us of those inconceivable numbers who had perished. And of those who were still to perish yet. I became uncontrollably morose, knowing I had been even a small part of the creation of this evil."

"The SS would not allow us to work at Birkenau, thank God. They did not want any witnesses to the heinous crimes they were committing there each hour. Instead, my barrack was assigned to manual labor repairing the camp at Auschwitz I."

"One day in early June, I was working with another newly arrived Pole moving construction lumber. These were large beams that should have had at least four men moving them. But myself and the other man, we struggled in our already half-starved state each day. We were taking the beams from a large pile and carrying them across the camp to the work site. We had moved four and were exhausted.

"Then it happened. As we were taking the next beam from the mountainous pile that we had to finish moving that day, the stacked lumber shifted. The pile came directly down on us in an instant, before I or the other man could move out of its way."

"I felt my lower leg snap as the beams fell on us. The pain was un-bearable. I lay with my leg broken pinned by three of the logs. I pushed my chest off the ground, my elbows behind me, so I could see better the condition of my leg. It was broken through the shin, angled under the weight of the wood. It was bent where it was not meant to bend."

"I could not stand the pain. I was crying out loud, and only now the guards were coming to see what had happened. I could hear them cursing in German as they came near. I turned my head to see the man who had been helping me."

"He was covered in the pile of beams up to his chest. It was clear his chest was caved in, blood was spewing from his mouth. I could hear him praying the Hail Mary over and over in Polish, each prayer came out slower than the time before. He began to choke on the blood in his throat. Now the guards were standing over us both."

"I remember the picture fading at that point as I was about to black out. I closed my eyes. I listened through the fog of pain. I could hear the guards discussing my partner, how he was already dying and wasn't worth wasting a bullet to take his life any sooner. However, I could hear them discuss me next, how I only had a broken leg, and how in my half-dead state I would never heal. The last sound I heard was a guard drawing his pistol from its leather holster. That was a sound I had heard many times before. It echoed like a church bell in my brain every time I heard it. It was the warning of impending, instantaneous death, feared even in this factory of death. My pain overpowered me, its black shroud was fastened tight over me. I thought I would not hear the shot that was to kill me."

"I awakened the next day back in the camp infirmary. I was surprised beyond belief to be there a second time. My cot faced the window looking over the grounds where we took roll call every morning. As I looked through the window, past the ground, I could see the graceful swaying of the willow. I was weak, weaker than before, and I suspect I was drugged. Everything seemed a blur. Once I was able to gain my wits, I looked to the left of me and saw a crust of bread on the table. Why were they doing this? Why did they keep me alive, wasting their medicine and food on a half corpse?"

"The answer came soon enough. Over the time I spent in the infirmary, I could hear the medical staff chatting. Did they not know I was fluent in German? Did they not care?"

"The Russians had now pushed the Germans back from the Soviet Union, and were driving them back through eastern Poland. At least what used to be eastern Poland. I could hear the staff discussing this with great fear. They knew the atrocities that the Germans had levied on the Russian people as they pushed their way to Leningrad, Moscow and Stalingrad. Now the Russians were fighting with an intensity that everyone in the Auschwitz complex feared as they drew closer."

"So they fed me and cared for me. Not for my human soul. Not for my Polish heart. But solely for my Russian tongue."

Chapter 17

STANLEY SAT IN the welcome darkness of his California hotel room, his face lighted only from the blue reflection of his laptop. He had just encrypted the latest transmission from Jean Paul.

It read:

"Have located and interviewed the prostitute Annette. Surprisingly, still in the working district of Amsterdam, along the canal, only a short walk from the Marquis Continental Hotel. I took this as a sign she needed money, or else I think she would have fled. I entered her canal-side parlor, and convinced her it would be more profitable to take a walk with me. She was afraid, but agreed when I doubled the offered sum to three thousand euros. I think she feared I was sent to detain her, possibly permanently. She was French, as apparently were the men for whom she worked. Her clients, she assured me, were from all nationalities."

"She stepped to the sidewalk, and spoke to a very rough-looking gentleman. I could hear her say in French she was coming to my hotel for one thousand euros. I assume she meant to pocket the rest. Dangerous play with the looks of this proprietor. She changed into some less provocative clothing."

"As we walked she relaxed somewhat. I put the thousand euros in her hand to calm her, and told her the other two would be paid when we completed

our walk. We spoke in French, and this relaxed her further, I thought."

"I told her I was being engaged by a friend of the Barber family, but that I was not police. I told her nothing she could tell me about that night could possibly be used in court. I lied, but it relaxed her further. I said the family only wanted to know what had happened. She agreed to tell me."

"She is a very attractive woman. Somewhat taller than most French, and very dark, even by French standards. I think she likely had some Algerian in her bloodline, but the effect was stunningly beautiful. Her accent was Marseilles, and I suspect the crime syndicate there brought her to Amsterdam to maximize their profits."

"She had been contacted by Mr. Barber through an intermediary at the hotel, most likely the concierge, though she never identified him directly. She came to Mr. Barber's room that night and liked him very much. She actually enjoyed the sex she had with him, as he was far from her typical clientele. He was good looking, athletic, and a very good lover by all counts. She assured me these are unexpected traits in her profession. Mr. Barber explained that he made it to Amsterdam several times a year and would like to set up a process for requesting her in advance. This they did through the intermediary."

"On Mr. Barber's next visit, a twist was introduced to the routine. When Annette got to the hotel room. Mr. Barber was accompanied by a young English woman named Cecily. That of course was our second deceased, Mr. Barber's love interest from the International Office in London, Miss Cecily Kendall. She was younger than Barber, noted Annette, but not indecently so. Barber explained he wished for Annette to spend the evening with Cecily and himself for this and future trips. Annette sensed the payday, tripled her normal overnight rate and Barber agreed instantly."

"On their first night together, it became clear to Annette that Cecily was not awkward with another woman, and this surely was an experience she had had before. Barber mostly watched, touching them as they were engaged, until he could no longer control himself. He would couple with Cecily, and Annette would caress and kiss both as they consumed each other. Very easy work by her standards."

"So it appears this satisfying of these forbidden pleasures was one which they felt they could not engage safely in the UK. So the trips continued."

"On the fifth encounter together, which happens to be the night of Barber's and Kendall's death, the routine was slightly different. Annette arrived at the hotel room to find only Ms. Kendall. Cecily explained that Mr. Barber was at a brief dinner meeting in the hotel, but she had Theodore's (as she called him) permission to start as soon as Annette arrived. They showered together first, and had moved to the bed."

"Annette was in the act of pleasing Miss Kendall when Mr. Barber entered the room, pardoning the interruption. Annette remembers how Mr. Barber liked to flash his American college French, which was very bad, she noted. He walked in on them, with a surprise bottle of Dom Pérignon and a plate of English strawberries remarking, 'J'ai les delicieux Strawberries d'Angleterre, et des champagnes des France.' Annette teased in English how she loved the fruit of the British, the wine of France, and the corruption of both in Mr. Barber's French. She returned to pleasuring Miss Kendall. Barber popped the champagne and set the strawberries on the bedside table. He watched as he disrobed, and Annette thought how this was bound to be a short night. Little did she know how correct she would be."

"She finished with Cecily, who whole-heartedly enjoyed every second of Annette's labors. She awaited Ted Barber's vices to satisfy, both knowing there were no vices in this city that were suppressed, so long as there was a profit to be made by it."

"Annette began to turn her talents on Mr. Barber, who pulled back, which was unusual. Totally disrobed, he explained he wanted to shower before round two began. All three drank the champagne in a hearty toast, consuming two thirds of the bottle. Mr. Barber explained to Ms. Kendall how the British strawberries had just been flown in, and were a gift of his (and for that matter her) firm's President, Mr. Powell. They had just finished dinner, and Annette heard Barber say that there was an opening in the organization that Mr. Powell had told Barber he would be perfect for."

"Annette said that Barber appeared excited at the prospect of returning to America, but Ms. Kendall was decidedly less so."

"Barber jumped into the shower. Annette began to feed the strawberries to Cecily, slowly rubbing the outline of her mouth with the fruit, and making Cecily snap upwards to get a bite. After consuming the first two berries, Miss Kendall grabbed one from the plate and walked into the bathroom to hand feed one to Mr. Barber in the shower. She came back to the bed, her arm doused by warm shower water, stumbling gently."

"Cecily plopped back into the bed in a forcibly unbecoming way. Annette hovered over her and began to plant small kisses on her beautifully young face. Cecily had loved this from their first embrace together, and usually responded with the soft moans of a forbidden rapture. Tonight her response was much more muted, and before long there was no response at all."

"Annette became very concerned. Cecily's breathing had become increasingly shallow. Annette began stroking her face, gently at first, but more forcibly until she finally began slapping Cecily hard with no apparent response. It appeared that her breathing had stopped totally at this point. Just then Mr. Barber emerged from the shower, dripping wet, making no attempt to dry himself. He stood bracing himself in the doorway, calling

for Cecily. He appeared drugged, slurring his words, fighting to control his breath and his movements."

"At this point Annette panicked. She moved, frightened, away from the quiet, still form of Ms. Kendall. Barber, struggling, worked his way to the bed. He attempted to revive Ms. Kendall, with no response. Annette threw her dress over her head as he did so and slipped out the door and down two flights of stairs barefooted. From my earlier interview with the head bellman in the lobby, I knew she had dashed out the front door and turned left into the maze of streets leading back to the red light district."

"I do not believe the police were advised of Annette's role in this by the hotel, but I am sure they will piece this together from the lobby security video."

"After Annette's dash through the lobby, she was soon followed by a dazed, bare chested Mr. Barber, emerging from the elevator, calling her name as he stumbled through the hotel lobby. He wore only his slacks, no shoes or socks. The doorman drew a very perturbed look from the night manager, and moved to intercept Mr. Barber at the hotel entrance. Barber threw him back violently, perhaps having trouble gauging his own force. He moved out into the narrow quiet streets. He turned right toward the nearest canal, calling Annette's name furiously. Cecily lay dying upstairs, if not already dead by that point, from the strawberries that we know from the toxicity reports of Mr. Barber and Miss Kendall were abundantly laced with cocaine. Barber was extremely allergic to this drug, so for him to even make the lobby, let alone the alleys of Amsterdam, was quite a feat."

"I suppose finding Cecily Kendall apparently dead at the hands of Annette upped his adrenaline levels. Mr. Barber made it to the footbridge that traversed the canal that runs along the Anne Frank Museum. He climbed atop the railing to look for Annette, lost his balance, and fell into the canal. He was heard struggling in the water, but his body became *lodged under the embankment, and he drowned. The police were called and initiated a search. His body was not found until the next morning by the police divers.*

"Miss Kendall's body was found that evening, dead from an apparent cocaine overdose. The remaining six strawberries were tested by the police, and found to have only traces of cocaine on their skins. By the amounts found in the remains of Mr. Barber and Miss Kendall, it appears only the top layer of berries were laced with the drug. Miss Kendall was unfortunate to have consumed the first few, which apparently were the most heavily laced. Mr. Barber likely only consumed a bite or two in the shower, based upon the contents of his stomach. His allergic reaction surely was violent, and played a major part in his drowning."

"One last point from the interview with Annette. Racing back to her parlor that evening, she laid low for some time. She thought of returning to Marseilles, but could not as her 'employer' would not release her."

"I did ask her why she herself had not consumed any of the drug laced fruit."

"'I suppose that was the touch of fate,' she responded."

"I asked what she meant."

"'I cannot eat fruit that has seeds. They get trapped in my insides and it is very painful. Strawberries are the worst, as their seeds are many, and are on the outside. It is a curse.'

"This woman was saved by her very curse. She suffers from diverticulitis. Because of this, she lived to tell the story of that evening."

Chapter 18

STANLEY COULD HEAR the raspy breath of his father. He was struggling to finish his story, for he could feel in his body that his time was very near. He continued to tell his son Stashew his tale in Polish.

"They came for me in the heat of early August of 1944. I was out of the infirmary, but my leg was not fully healed and was tied to a splint."

"Once again I was loaded into a vehicle, this time the back seat of an open army staff car. The front seat was occupied by Keller, who was driving, and in the passenger seat was another guard. They were preoccupied, they seemed under the weight of something ominous. Were the Russians on the verge of overtaking them? They did not talk. They were nervously silent in their thoughts."

"Keller drove through the gate of Auschwitz, once more beneath the sign saying in German, 'Work will set you free.' A lie to those who entered there, it came to be truly ironic in my case. Yet, to this day, my Stashew, I have never really been free. You will understand why shortly."

"I later understood their orders were to go to Warsaw. This was something of a death sentence for them. It was delivering these two men into the crucible of fate. It was the vessel into which one soul would be sacrificed, while another, though lost forever, remained alive."

"Warsaw had been the site of a massive uprising by the Polish underground starting on the 1st of August in what was now 1944. The city had been in the control of the Nazis for nearly five years now, and this uprising was unexpected and unusually well-organized. It was timed with the anticipated advancement of the Red Army into the eastern suburbs of Warsaw, across the Vistula River. The old town of Warsaw, and the bulk of the city, lie on the west bank of the Vistula. The Red Army had pushed the Germans past the old Russian/Polish border on the 13th of July."

"On August 1st, the Polish Underground began Operation Tempest, expecting support from the Red Army from across the Vistula. The river could have been an ocean. The Russians sat on its banks and watched, offering almost no support whatsoever to the insurrection."

"The rebellion was quick to take ground in central Warsaw from the Nazis. The Germans lost 8,000 troops to the underground by the end of the revolt, with almost an equal number of Nazis wounded. But the Russians did not come across the river, except for 1,200 Polish army troops they commanded and released to cross the Vistula. The battle would rage on for 63 days, and by the middle of August was stalemated near the old town section of Warsaw. This is the area that became the crucible – the *Stare Miasto*."

"Keller and the other SS officer barely spoke until Keller made an unexpected turn thirty minutes after leaving the camp."

"'What are you doing? This is not the route to Warsaw.' began the companion in German."

"'I am sweeping west, in case the communists have come across the River,' Keller responded."

"I knew where Keller was headed, and I hoped to God the treasure he sought had been moved. I proved to be terribly wrong. Later, the car pulled onto the farm road outside of Katowice. It was the farm where Keller's conquest had been interrupted by the local Wehrmacht. Today, he was of a single mind not to be interrupted."

"'Why are you pulling into this farm, we need to be headed to Warsaw. We will be found in dereliction of our orders. We will be shot.' stated the other guard."

"'We need fuel if we will make it to Warsaw. This old dog has the fuel we need. I have been here before. Trust me,' said Keller."

"'You have two cans in the back. If you did not come this far west, we could have gotten there. I doubt that this farm has any fuel at all. What are you up to?' the other SS guard demanded of Keller, clearly agitated."

"The car pulled into the dirt area outside the farm house. Keller told me to yell in Polish that if the old man did not come out, he would burn the farm.

"I did so. Keller had stopped the car and now moved to the two cans of fuel in the trunk. As he began to take out the cans, the other officer got out of the vehicle."

"'I will not allow you to waste this fuel to burn a peasant farm. What is the matter with you?' the guard yelled in a very animated voice."

"Keller insisted I yell out in Polish again that the farm was about to be burned. The old Polish farmer emerged reluctantly from his farmhouse."

"Keller told me to ask for her, or he would burn the farm. The other guard was continuing to protest to Keller in German. He ordered Keller to put the can down. Keller did so. The Polish farmer stood at the base of his farm house steps."

"The second guard ran to me, looked me in the eyes and told me to tell the farmer to return inside. I sat in the back of the vehicle, my leg throbbing. He stared into my eyes, and in German yelled, 'Now. Tell this old man to go inside now.'

"He was yelling at me as Keller pulled his Luger. I watched as he released the safety with his thumb and pointed it at the base of the skull of the second guard."

"The explosion shocked me even as I was expecting it. The muzzle of the Luger was but an inch away from the guard's neck. Keller squeezed the trigger and the force of the blast was staggering."

"The guard was still looking in my eyes as the side of his skull fragmented across the back seat of the car. I saw the surprise in his eyes as the click of the trigger preceded the blast. Then all was silent save the echo of the woods. His blood and brains splattered across me and the seat I was constrained in."

"Keller drew his breath. I suspect he had just killed his first German. But he was determined to get the girl. This time nothing would stop him. It was rare that he was released from the camp, and he was headed to possible death in Warsaw. He wanted the girl. He would have the girl."

My father cringed in physical pain, or was it merely the revulsion of the memory he was retelling?

"At the sound of the gunshot, she came out of hiding in the woods surrounding the house. She looked at me, already crying. She recognized me. Her look of pity for my skeletal face, bizarrely blended in with her fear. She recognized Keller. She recognized the terror that was to come."

"Keller took her and tied her hands, throwing her into the car next to me. He was possessed. The father was yelling in Polish for me to tell him she was his only daughter, and not to take her away from him. He urged me to plead with Keller. I could tell him nothing. His daughter burrowed her head into my chest in the back seat of the car, afraid to see what was coming next.

"Keller raised his pistol, shooting at the old man across the dirt yard. He hit him in the shoulder above the heart he was aiming for. The old man spun round as the bullet penetrated and hit the front side of his shoulder blade. His daughter heard his howl of pain, and sobbed into the roughness of my camp shirt."

"Keller walked over to the old man as he attempted to crawl toward the car his daughter was in. Keller walked to him, leaned over and stepped on the back of his leg."

"Keller yelled to me in German, 'Translate this, and do not change a word, or I will kill you here and now.'

"I did not wait for the words in German. I knew the Nietzsche quote that his devil heart craved. Its ceremony heightened his sensation of the killing."

"I said to him in Polish, '*Beware when you wrestle with a monster, that you may become a monster yourself.*'

"This old man was no monster, just trying to protect his young daughter. Or were the words meant for me? A warning to roll from my own tongue in my own language?"

"The shot rang out. The old man's body lay still. The daughter's sobbing into my chest became uncontrollable. I thought of my years with Keller. *'When you stare into the abyss, the abyss also stares into you,'* I said in German, for his effect."

My father's tears were now streaming down his face, emaciated by cancer. It was as if he were back in the rear seat of that car in 1944. It was as if he were trying to wash the memory clean so he could pass peaceably from this life.

"Keller came to the car, and opened the door, dragging the girl across me with the force of a starving beast about to rip into its kill. He threw her into my lap, her legs outside the car. She screamed aloud, but was still stunned by witnessing her father's execution. He pulled her peasant dress up onto her back. There and then he raped her for the first time as she lay across my lap. I could feel his every thrust, transferred through her young body, pushing against my starved near corpse. As I held her sobbing, young face in my arms, he raped her violently."

"I had seen so much death and torture in my time in Auschwitz, I had feared I had become numb. But in the matter of minutes I watched as two men were coldly murdered solely so Keller could rape this girl, I felt my blood surge in my veins. All I could do, though, was watch as she sobbed into my lap as he took her. I feared he would kill her next, but she would not be that lucky."

"As he raped her, I held her as tight as I could, and through her sobbing whispered to her that it would soon be over."

"I stroked her face, but there was no consolation. Her profusive tears dripped from my bone fingers. The tears would find no refuge, only the cracked, dried skin stretching a morbid yellow arc across my broken frame."

"I realized her horror in full at that point. Her father dead, she was being forcibly raped by his murderer across the lap of a skeleton, who asked her to believe in his own lie."

"'This will soon be over.' I whispered to her in Polish."

"Keller finished, turned his back to us both as he pulled up his trousers. He then grabbed her roughly, and shackled her to me. He was not done with her."

"Keller was saving her for Warsaw. He was taking us both into the crucible. She was somehow his release, his last sensation of power, of domination. And through my tongue, I was his only hope of survival. The Germans feared the Russians would cross the Vistula, and enter the fray. He needed my Russian, as much as his vulgar flesh needed the horrid domination of the girl. He was a devilish mixture of gluttony and fear. Which made this bastard extremely dangerous."

"He was taking us both into the hell of battle and insurrection that Warsaw had become. In that deadly environment, the flames of the fires of the past forged the iron will of the secrets of today."

Chapter 19

THE FLIGHT TO London had been uneventful on the Gulf-stream. Stanley sat across the table from Powell, who was clearly preoccupied as the selection by the Board of Directors drew near in a matter of days. There was no engaging in small talk. Powell was cold and felt no need to dally in now unneeded, social small talk. There were four others on the manifest, and he treated them in an equally frigid manner. We were all his subordinates, and his actions reinforced that fact. He barely spoke to them, quite frankly, because there was no need to.

Stanley had reflected on the hours leading up to the flight. He had filed his report with Marlow. Stanley had served the function he had been requested to serve. The Board of Directors was meeting in three days. Their selection would be made public on Thursday. The report in the hands of Marlow would be poured over by Marc Constantine and Everett Roberts during the very hours that Stanley accompanied Langston Powell across the Atlantic.

The remainder of the funds from the firm would be in his account by Monday morning. Knowing this, Stanley could not resist looking across the jet's table at Powell. Did he know he was the opportunity that Stanley had feared would never present itself in his life? Powell sat quietly alone among them, consuming his work. His only concession to the lengthy flight was to have donned a pair of reading glasses that reflected the warm glow of the low cabin lights as the night chilled black outside the cabin. These "cheaters" sat condescendingly low on his nose, allowing him to rip through the contents of the thick portfolio that had been expressly prepared to consume his excess energy by his handlers, a tactic learned out of self-preservation.

But it was the last discussion that Stanley had with Powell that made him finalize what was to go into the report to Marlow. In Powell's office on Saturday, the day before leaving California, they began discussing the future of the Daedalus Destroyer program. This discussion crystallized Stanley's action.

Powell was revealed to Stanley in his totality. Stanley would see Langston Powell as a man consumed. Consumed by power, consumed by winning, consumed by being better than anyone he ever would come in contact with. If that came at the cost of a few Aerospace executive's careers, that was one thing. When the cost was to be the very freedom Powell purported to protect through the Daedalus Destroyers aloft, Stanley knew what he had to do.

Powell sat behind his cherry-stained desk probing his email one last time that Saturday afternoon. He was dressed casually in gray slacks and a form-fitting, maroon golf shirt, with a championship status logo proudly on display. Powell was very fit, his face tight and flush with power.

"What a wonderful perk from this office to have access to an executive jet, especially for international travel," Stanley remarked. He sat in Powell's office this afternoon, lean but paunchy by comparison to Powell. He felt his age from the immediate past week's travels, and the weight of what was to come was already bearing down on him.

"Stanley, the firm provides the Gulfstream, the limos, and the other perks to maximize my contributions to taking this firm into a very profitable future. The perks, the salary, the bonuses are all their attempts to retain me. Why are they so anxious to retain me – because they know I have seen the future, and I know how to steer this beloved enterprise through its jagged passages."

Stanley was perplexed, and showed it in his face. He was anticipating more to follow and Powell did not fail him. Out of habit, Stanley wiped his long, gray locks with his left hand, palm outward, cocking his head slightly. Powell smirked, as the cocked head gesture reminded him of the quizzical stare of his Irish Setter at home. "Where does one pick up such an unprofessional gesture?", Powell wondered to himself.

"I am lost," began Stanley. "Sure the Daedalus Destroyer Program is profitable, but how many drones can the CIA need for the Global War on Terror?"

"Stanley, let me explain," continued Powell. "Drones are today's instruments of the security forces, with specific missions – reconnaissance, reconnoiter, weapons launch. Weapons in the Global War on Terror – GWOT. But in the future, these platforms will become much more than that, they will be infrastructure – as ubiquitous as highways and bridges. Thousands will be continuously flying over the skies of our own country and the rest of the world in pre-planned, round the clock routing, allowing persistent intelligence gathering."

"Domestic War on Terror?" Stanley quipped.

Powell had his reading glasses in hand now, and used them to illustrate his points. "Yes, Stanley. Exactly. Our security will depend on the continuous collection of data by the ever-present network of these platforms linked directly to the NSA, FBI, and CIA. Not just today's electronic eavesdropping, but data that can track the movement of millions through cell phone and an ever-increasing network of integrated video collection."

"Sounds very totalitarian, Langston. But doesn't that already exist today. I thought Snowden and Wiki leaks had proved that."

Stanley's response indicated he did not fully comprehend the vision. Powell felt the need to spell it out for all those who lacked the vision, Stanley among them.

"Stanley, I can also see the day where these systems will also be weaponized to take out immediate threats even in our own skies. It will start across the wide expanses of our American West. Perhaps a gruesome terror attack that comes from across the border. The American people will be demanding protection. That protection will come from the Daedalus Destroyers. Quietly collecting the information to keep us safe. Before long a Daedalus Destroyer takes out a car full of terrorists about to strike. Once done, it is only a matter of time before they are accepted across the more populated portions of our country. The East Coast, Washington DC, protected by our drones."

Now Stanley felt it was time to interrupt the frightful image that Powell was projecting. He started, "Given that scenario, it's only a matter of time before our enemies use these very weapons against our cities themselves. Electronically hijack the platforms and command them to fire on the very citizens they were designed to protect?"

Stanley could not suppress this response, and could see not only the immediate rage in Powell's eyes, but the grinding of his clenched jaw, as well. The vision of the all-powerful dared to be opposed.

"It's only the novices like you who do not see the opportunity in selling the government the security software to prevent this scenario from ever happening. In addition to the drones, the integration software, the ground control stations and the weapons eventually. As well as perpetual upgrades. Who will refuse to pay to stay safe? It's coming Stanley. The days of Utopian bliss are long gone. Wrap your mind around it. It will provide for the safety of this country. And unlike satellites, will be affordable in large numbers flying below the air traffic routes. Trust me, it is coming."

Langston's eyes were narrow slits now, his words hard and meant for impact.

"Stanley, the world is changing. Shrinking. And in that tightening sphere, the friction of deadly terror becomes more concentrated. Is it disfavorable to you that I see this coming, and am preparing our great company to provide the solutions and systems that our government will need to maintain our way of life?"

Stanley cringed at the self-deception that Powell was spewing.

"Langston, I am very confident that no matter what comes to pass in the near future, you will be able to guide this firm to profit from it."

Langston held up both arms in victory, his glasses now pointing to the ceiling. "Stanley," he said smiling broadly. "That is exactly my job. I could not have put it better."

Stanley continued, "But in the very actions you describe, our way of life will be destroyed, not protected."

"You are too late, Stanley," Powell said. "The future I describe is already on its way. We will live free of the fear of terrorists. American lives will be saved." Langston Powell saw the future, and it was profitable.

But that was yesterday afternoon. This Sunday evening, they were now working their way over Newfoundland en route to London. Stanley looked about the jet. Powell had almost spoken to no one, just absorbing himself in the briefing papers laid out before him on the table. Or perhaps he was consumed thinking of the Board of Director's selection – the prize that now was just outside of his reach?

This man, who he flew with through the night onward to Europe, what would he stop at to make his vision become reality? Hardly anything, Stanley concluded. The same conclusion that Constantine, Roberts and Marlow had reached when they asked themselves that very question. They knew he was capable of being culpable in the Barber drowning, and Stanley's research had demonstrated just that.

Stanley still wondered if Marlow was actually aligned with Powell, behind the scenes. Constantine and Roberts had entrusted him greatly in dealing with me, but if Powell was to be the next CEO, then Marlow could be handsomely rewarded for sharing his confidences. Had the contents of the report Stanley had submitted to Marlow late last night already found its way into Langston Powell's hands? Did Powell know of the judgment that Stanley had rendered on him?

Stanley decided to try and sleep as the Gulfstream pressed through the night onto London. How ironic that Powell was to be in the International Office in the morning, the very office run by Ted Barber until his death. Stanley thought of the events he would be undertaking in London tomorrow while Powell visited triumphantly the domain of the late Ted Barber.

There had not yet been a permanent head of office named. Barber's second-in-command still acted in his permanent absence. Stanley could not help but wonder as he dozed off if Powell's business in London was to somehow take advantage of this situation?

Stanley was awakened as they flew over Ireland in the beautiful morning light. The cabin steward was preparing breakfast for the half-dozen executives. They were busy dressing and shaving for the meeting scheduled for them immediately after they cleared customs. Powell appeared in a beautiful blue-striped shirt, complete with French cuffs with black onyx and yellow gold cuff links, after visiting the head. His gray cashmere and wool suit jacket was in his hand. Stanley could not mistake the label – Yves St. Laurent.

"Stanley," Powell stated a few seconds later, "You can come to the International Office if you like, but I thought you might prefer to spend the day touring London. You can take the car in with us. We'll drop you at Trafalgar Square. Just be back at the hotel no later than six this evening. We'll have an early dinner tonight and tomorrow morning we'll be wheels up for Poznan at 6:30 AM. I don't want to leave my skeptical interpreter behind." The word *skeptical* was turned like a card in its delivery.

Powell's face was hard. No trace of the wide smiles and executive charms lavished out in his office. It was as if a switch was flipped. He had gotten me on that plane, and now there was no need for pleasantries.

Langston had the limousine that picked them up at the terminal work its way toward their office in Central London near Oxford Street. It was only a few blocks from the American Embassy. After the rest of the executives departed for their meetings, Langston stuck his head back into the limo and looked Stanley in the eye. His face was flush with a sarcastic grin, shared between the privacy of the two men alone.

"Since your heavy lifting is over now, relax a little and take in the sights. I want you fresh for our meetings with the Polish government on Wednesday and Thursday." Langston winked on the words *heavy lifting*. He flashed a shallow grin that quickly went flat against his hard countenance.

Did Langston know what Stanley had submitted to Marlow? Now Stanley was sure of it, but decided not to press the issue, as Powell would surely have said the *heavy lifting* was referring to the INAR review.

The driver crawled in the congestion down to Trafalgar Square. Stanley exited the limo and walked across the intersection to a coffee shop he had frequented in the past. At 10 AM, he walked back across the intersection, stepped briskly past the Nelson Column Monument and its guard of bronze heraldic lions. Climbing the stairs, he stepped directly into the National Gallery. After walking up the interior staircase, he turned to his right and entered the Post-Impressionist Art Gallery. It was still very early and the room was all but empty.

He fixed his gaze on the Van Gogh treatment of two crabs, marveling at his own knowledge at how perfectly the artist captured the fusion of reds and whites of the creatures, one upturned. The background brought a fusion of green hues touched with yellow in broad, masterful brushstrokes.

Stanley stood transfixed at the painting for 30 minutes, as he had planned. He enjoyed the close inspection of the art, as one does when exploring the face of a long-forgotten friend. The time passed quickly, and then he began his pre-planned procession.

He walked down Whitehall towards Parliament, past the Horse

Guards Palace, noting the clock over the entry to the Parade grounds, with the infamous black dot on the clock face near the two. This was the subtle, British way to remark that when Charles I was beheaded across the street on a scaffold at 2 PM, it was a black mark on the collective pride of the British people.

Deposing a monarch was a watershed moment for a culture. Beheading one was even more calamitous. Stanley could sense the moment in history. The people could not muster the courage to do this themselves, even after years of civil war. So the Parliamentarian Roundheads did the dirty business for them. Once done, it could not be undone. Not by the people years later throwing out the Lord Protector's son, and bringing back the monarch's son. Not by re-embracing a hollowed-out, figurehead monarchy to present day. Love the queen as they may, that dirty little black dot still stood shamefully at two o'clock.

Stanley saw Powell in his ascending role as Lord Protector of the future of democracy. A Lord Protector who would stop at nothing to achieve his vision. And like the lost head of a monarch, what is done cannot be undone.

The vision had to be stopped before it was realized.

Stanley made Westminster Square a few minutes later and immediately dropped into the Underground. He took several tubes, five to be exact, to assure he had not been followed. Over an hour later, he surfaced in the area east of Canary Wharf, and once assuring again that he hadn't been tailed, he walked into the headquarters of Barclay's Bank. He had to prepare for his rendezvous with Jean Paul later today here in London, and more importantly, Friday in Warsaw's Old Town – *Stare Miasto*.

Chapter 20

HIS FATHER'S VOICE was weakened to the point of collapse by the strain of the tale. Each word seemed to drain the life from him, leaving only the suspense of whether his father would finish the tale before he passed into the peaceful relief of the afterlife.

Stanley heard his father breathe a deep breath, deep compared to the shallow draws he had had been taking. He was bracing himself for the telling of this final part of the tale.

"I asked you to make three promises, and today you will know why. I ask you first to always be proud you are Polish, to love and look after your mother, and to defend the weak from the strong throughout your life."

"*Stare Miasto* – Warsaw's Old Town, was the area of the heaviest fighting during Operation Tempest, and this is where the girl and I were taken by Keller. Our drive to Warsaw from Katowice was surreal, sunny and externally peaceful, interrupted only by the progression of troops and battle scars that increased as we neared Warsaw. The girl was nestled up against my shoulder, never stopping her crying, never looking up. She dared not look at the man Keller who had torn her father and her childhood away from her."

"As we came into Warsaw, the devastation was incredible. We drove east past the brick walls of the Jewish Ghetto, drained empty by Birkenau's ghastly and immoral efficiency. We passed several more checkpoints. At each, the soldiers would inspect Keller's papers, ask who we were, and after noting the Skull and Crossbones of Keller's SS Totenkopf uniform, allowed him to press deeper into the insurgency zone."

"The town wore the years of occupation as a gray film, weighty but freshly pierced with the life breath of resistance. It was not visible yet, but was felt in the breach of confidence of the oppressors. They knew the insurrection would be crushed, but was it only a preparation for the end? The specter of the Red Army raised from across the river."

Stanley thought he noted his father's soul rise as he told this portion of the tale. It gave him a brief energy, however slight, that very rapidly waned as the tale continued.

"Finally, we were on the edge of the old town. The area was surely now a war zone. The Polish underground had fought bravely, but as the Soviets were now on the other side of the Vistula and showed no interest in supporting their insurgency, the Polish Underground fighters were surrounded by the now constantly reinforced German army."

"Nothing was normal, as I had recalled on my visits as a boy to this beautiful ancient town of Warsaw. Now, the walls of houses and buildings in this area were partially torn down, the loose bricks settling in disarray at their base. The insides were often exposed to the streets. The fighting was house to house, rubble to rubble. The Poles, betrayed by the Red Army, were fighting for their collective life, and it was clear no allies were coming to assist them. Only the vengeance of the German Wehrmacht was coming – raging to teach the insurgents the full measure of the terror they had ignited."

"Keller took the girl and myself to a courtyard that had been partially destroyed. He chained me in shackles around my frail waist to a pipe that was still very firmly secured to the back wall of the building. I would try for the next several days to release myself from this prison but with no success. My hands were tied tight with leather bindings that cut to the bones of my starved, skeletal hands. The girl was secured through my waist shackles, handcuffed so tightly that her delicate wrists bled at the slightest movement. Then it was revealed what we were being saved for."

"I will be nearby," Keller said, "so don't try to escape. Tell the girl what you like, but she is here for me, for my pleasure. You think she sees you as a protector, but she will hate you for passively watching as her father was killed. And for your interrogation of the Polish insurgents that I will bring here in the days ahead. And for watching as I take her again and again."

"With these cold words, he bent her over, her hands cuffed to my waist manacle, her ragged dress up across her back and raped her again. Her face was full of anguish. She cried but no longer sobbed. She held tight to me, and with my finger I stroked the tears from her face, and whispered tenderly in Polish, 'It will soon be over.'

"Even as this was ongoing, I could hear the fighting. It was very close, and very intense. As much as the raping of my young, country maiden's innocence sickened me, the sounds of Polish resistance emboldened me. I knew then that I would have to find the strength to fight back in some way."

Chapter 21

THE FOLLOWING FRIDAY found them in Warsaw. Beautiful sunny, brisk Warsaw.

Four days after London, Stanley strolled aside a smiling, jovial Langston Powell through the beauty of the open, green Łazienki Park in Warsaw. They walked along the path leading to the Palace on the Water, a beautiful, seventeenth century white palace surrounded by water - canals on both sides, and a large pond in the front and rear. The water washed right up to the structure, lapping peacefully against its white palace walls.

In the summer, tourists rode covered, gondola-shaped boats bearing swan likenesses in circles around the large pond. But this was November, and the chill of the fall had driven away the boats, leaving behind a placid, mirrored pond reflecting the Water Palace among the willows. Stanley could not help but think how the canals of Amsterdam were as peaceful as this scene in the light of day, but became an accessory to death in the darkness of night.

Gentle ripples softly kissed the stuccoed palace walls. The sun beamed joyously through the crystal blue sky. It was only Stanley and Langston, walking slowly abreast.

"Stanley, I couldn't be in better hands than yourself today for this tour of Warsaw. I really appreciate your taking the time to do this," Powell said as he laid his heavy hand on Stanley's shoulder. "Especially after your performance in Poznan Wednesday and yesterday."

"I did nothing but interpret. That's what you brought me along for." Stanley replied modestly. He added heavily "I observe and translate. It is what I do."

It was a false modesty, but a true confession of a life's work. Langston Powell knew it also."

"Stanley, I brought you to interpret Polish to English. But you were more brilliant reading their body language, facial expressions, and responses to every proposal we made. Your comments to me during the negotiations saved us from cutting the cost of our proposal by at least three million dollars U.S. It was worth every penny to bring you along. I was told that you read people masterfully, and it showed in Poznan."

So the jabs began as pats on the back, like the opening round of a championship prize fight with two contestants feeling each other out.

I was told that you could read people masterfully rang in his ears. The same words Everett Roberts had used the Monday before last. Stanley could see Powell's eyes probing his withered face for a response. It was a response Stanley denied Langston the pleasure of.

Powell continued, "Now I get a guided tour of one of Eastern Europe's loveliest capitals." Langston was absolutely beaming. Global Defense Analytics had just announced publicly the day before that Langston Powell would succeed the retiring COO, and he would also succeed Everett Roberts as CEO in 9 months. Stanley had cleared him of wrongdoing in his report to Marlow.

Stanley intentionally did not let on that he knew Powell's ascension had been announced, and wanted to see how long it would be before Langston raised the topic.

"This city is absolutely glorious," Powell effused.

Stanley smiled, agreeing.

Then Powell added, "Even if it is the Epcot version…"

"I am sorry, Langston, I don't understand your comment." Stanley was stunned he would be so disrespectful of his country's heritage.

"Stanley," Langston replied in an extended broad smirk, attempting to be disarmingly casual. He raised his hands as if to say, "What? You don't understand?"

He continued, "Stan, come on, I did my homework. You know me, I am all about research. The Germans destroyed 85% of this city in World War II. They were retaliating for the Polish uprisings during the war. What the fighting with the insurgents didn't bring down, the Germans systematically destroyed to punish the Poles in the short period after the insurgency. It was all rebuilt years later, taking donor bricks from deconstructed cities elsewhere in Poland. Come on Stanley, if you're going to give me a guided tour, don't leave out half the story." Another jab.

"Yes, the Nazis destroyed over 85% of this beautiful city on Hitler's personal orders to punish the Poles for the 63-day uprising. It would take nearly 63 years to rebuild. The Poles rebuilt it faithfully from photos and architectural plans. Other Polish cities and towns be-came brick donors to rebuild the capital. But their names I would not expect you to know, let alone be able to pronounce." Stanley was now jabbing back. "Your reference to Disney is not a good analogy. While Epcot does give visitors a condensed snapshot to the cultures of the world, and one that I personally enjoyed, the rebuilding of Warsaw was done brick for brick, window for window, house for house, square for square. The Poles poured their hearts into rebuilding the city. Every brick a fiber in the cultural fabric these earnest souls clung to. Their hearts were their loom."

They had walked halfway around the swan pond along the footpath, and had reached the modest apex of the footbridge exactly opposite the water palace. Powell used his smart phone to capture the scene's tranquil beauty.

Stanley leaned close to his ear. "This, friend, was not destroyed. The photo you take is of an original."

Langston turned his head to look into Stanley's eyes. "Stanley, you never cease to amaze me. What else do you hide beneath that stoic exterior?"

Stanley pressed forward, "The Germans tried to erase the Polish culture completely. When they failed, the communists tried to suppress it even further. But they all failed. The Polish culture continues today, even if it was rebuilt in most sections of Warsaw. You see, this culture survived for 123 years before the first World War, when the *country* of Poland technically did not exist. Numerous partitions of Poland between Austria, Russia and Prussia took place in the late 1700's, even after what occurred in 1683."

"Okay, Stanley. You insist on proving to me you know more about Poland than I could research in a few hours." Powell responded, "I give. What was the big event in 1683?"

Stanley looked at Langston quizzically. "Perhaps your research was not as deep as you thought. There is a deep chasm between reading facts and understanding a culture. 1683 was a pivotal year in European and religious history. The Ottoman Turks invaded from the south, until Vienna lay sieged. The Muslim crescent threatened to replace the Christian crosses of Vienna. The Turks had Vienna sieged for long enough to tunnel right up to the walls of the city and were threatening to break through when the forces under the control of Polish King Jan Sobieski routed the Turks and drove them back from Austria and most of eastern Europe. To this day, this was the deepest penetration of the Muslims into Europe, further than the Moors in Western Europe. Also, to this day, the train that runs from Poland to Vienna is named the Jan Sobieski, in honor of this cultural rescue."

They had left the Water Palace behind them, walking along the trails of the park. It was a short walk to the Belvedere Palace. The Polish spelling was Belwedere, as there is no v in the Polish alphabet. It was the beautiful palace where the president of Poland resides, but likely more famous for adorning the Belvedere Vodka bottle throughout the world. Stanley had explained how it had once belonged to the Polish kings.

As they walked, the cool chill of the November wind rustled around them. It was a prelude of the bitter winter to come.

Langston Powell reflected on the history lesson. "Well, Stanley, the fact that the Austrians, Russians and Germans overran the country for over 100 years can only mean that the country was weak. The strong will always overrun the weak. That is exactly why we are here helping the Poles build up their defenses today."

"And some cash, Langston. Thanks to me, maybe three million more than it needed to be. Not quite as altruistic as you made it sound."

This drew a notably dire glance from Powell.

"Indeed the strong still take advantage of the weak." Stanley echoed aloud. "History continues to prove the strong always take advantage of the weak." He could hear echoes of his father.

As they continued their walk through Łazienki Park, they came upon a flight of marble steps, which they climbed. Atop was a landing featuring a beautiful fountain, at the end of which stood a large bronze statue of Frederic Chopin under the bend of a willow tree. The statue, including the bronze tree, sparkled with life under the afternoon sun. A concert piano on a nearby stage was sheltered from the weather by an awning of canvas tied off to a very modern aluminum frame.

"This is the world-famous statue dedicated to Frederic Chopin. Nothing captures the Polish soul more than a Chopin waltz or nocturne. His music was poetry written on a piano keyboard. Its expressiveness is unmatched in the history of music." Stanley rested, expecting the counterpoint of Powell.

"Yes, beautiful music, I agree. Although I am partial to Beethoven or Mozart, even Tchaikovsky or Rachmaninoff." Powell could not be expected to be agreeable to Stanley's perspective.

Stanley found it curious that he chose German, Austrian and Russian composers to make his point. This surely was intentional, a dig at the three countries that partitioned Poland.

Powell paused for a breath and then continued. "Actually Chopin was half French, half Polish. His most productive years were after he left Poland for the West. So you see Stanley, for the Poles to claim him outright is misguided."

Stanley took the insult, but pressed on in response. "Langston, make that argument to any Pole, and they will tell you the reason he was so productive in the West was the longing he had for the land where he was born and raised. He left Poland just before the failed revolution of 1830, and was received as a genius in Western Europe. While, yes, it is true he is buried in Paris, it is also true that his sister had his heart removed from his remains and brought back to Warsaw, where to this day it is interred in the Church of the Holy Cross. While he may have played so famously with his fingers, it was the longing for his native Poland in his heart that created the beauty of his music."

While Stanley gazed upon the Chopin monument, he could hear the nocturne that was not being played. He heard it in the mind of himself forty years ago. In a row house in Baltimore, in Fells Point, on Shakespeare Street, in a darkened bedroom his father lay dying, trying to tell the young Stanley a terrible truth, while Chopin's Nocturnes played somberly in the background.

"Stashew," his father continued with great effort, exhausting him. "My son, I sat chained to that pipe in that courtyard, the girl lay against me, her handcuffs laced through my waist manacles. The only movement we had was to slide up and down the pipe, to stand or to sit. The area around us was still a war zone. The Nazis were driving the Polish insurgents back into the Old Town area. We could hear the mortars and gunfire nearby. The girl trembled in my arms continuously. Then she stopped suddenly, looked up at my face and said to me with tears streaming down her face, 'I am sorry.'

"I could not believe she was apologizing to me, this beautiful young woman who this horrible Nazi continued to rape, all while she was confined to me by chains. I told her she had no reason to be sorry for this. She looked into me, her tears now outright sobs, 'No, not for what he has done to me, but for all they have done to you.'

"It was only then that I realized exactly how frail, how much a skeleton I had become over the past several years. She had not seen those who were starved to death, or mere days from it. She had not seen the mass killing of innocent Jews at Auschwitz and Birkenau, the incredible cruelty of the Nazis exacted on all. But it dawned on me that at that moment, at that second, that she also had not seen the life in my eyes. My eyes were tired, tired of watching cruelty by the strong at the expense of the weak, and not doing anything at all."

"It was then I realized as weak as I was, I had to do something."

The face sank deeper into frailty. A cold darkness coalesced behind it.

"The mortars were coming closer. The gunfire also. An hour or so had gone by with the girl in my arms heaving, crying tears not for what was to be done to her, but for what had been done to me."

"Suddenly a mortar round screamed over the courtyard and slammed into the wall high above the heads of us both. We were both terribly startled, and trembled waiting for the next round that did not come. I made sure she was not injured, and I had only been bruised and lightly cut by falling fragments of brick. After a few minutes, we struggled to our feet to see if we could move the pipe we were attached to. But no, the pipe was still secure, we were still trapped."

"As we brushed the brick debris off ourselves, there were several sharp fragments of brick. While not large enough to use as a weapon, I began to work the sharp edge of the brick against the leather strap constraining my wrists. I would use the very bonds of my captivity to attack Keller."

His father could no longer fight to tell the rest of the story this afternoon. He looked exhausted and scared. Stanley feared the cancer was waiting across the river, but for how long?

"My lovely Stashew," his father cried softly in his native Polish. "I must rest now. I must take a rest from the fear." His crying intensified, the tears crept cautiously down the sides of his face in rivulets, only to strengthen, joined into streams.

Stanley moved forward in an action that was unfamiliar to him. As much as he loved his dying father, he had to force himself forward to embrace his weeping face in the warmth of his palms, gently wiping away the tears. In the darkened daylight of his father's bedroom, he thought that it would soon be over, though he wouldn't say it out loud.

"Father," Stanley said in his softest tone, "It is the past. Do not fear it. It is gone."

His father's eyes, still weeping profusely, searched his son's face. "My Stashew," his breath no more than a shudder of an exhale, "It is not gone. I do not fear the past."

There was a very lengthy pause.

"What I fear is that it will follow me to where I now must go."

His father collapsed into a deep sleep. Stanley stood over him, assuring him that he was breathing, although shallowly. He needed to get out into the light of day, to wash clean this remembrance of death upon his own father's deathbed. He needed to feel the sun on his face.

Stanley's next decision, to take his often practiced neighborhood cobblestone walk to clear his mind, he would forever regret. When he returned to the home, his aged mother was weeping and bent in sorrow over the lifeless form of her husband. Stanley only then realized that fate doesn't often accommodate the needs of life. Stanley, thirty years old and strong, trembled uncontrollably and wept as he knelt at the bedside, next to his father's suddenly peaceful body. His father's fight to finish his tale was now lost forever to the release of death itself.

But thankfully, so was his father's pain in its retelling.

It would be ten years later when his mother was able to share the rest of the story with Stanley. It was a peaceful afternoon. They sat in the garden his father had built for her in the sunlight drinking warm tea. The most life-changing events are often cloaked in comfort, to lure one in. As these things go, it was totally unexpected.

Stanley's mind left his parents' memories and came back to Langston Powell's tour of Warsaw. They had left the park and walked up the *Nowy Świat* or New World Street. This formed part of the Royal Route, linking with the Krakowskie Przedmieście, or Krakow Promenade. Along the *Nowy Świat*, near the point it changed into the Krakowskie Przedmieście, they passed the statue of Copernicus. Powell started recounting his research.

Langston Powell took the opportunity to chip away at Stanley's beloved culture.

"The Poles so love their native sons, Stanley. Copernicus dared to challenge the Church by insisting that the earth revolved around the sun, and not all bodies revolved around the Earth as the Church had taught instead. The Church considered this heresy, for which they rather nastily put people to death. Is that not right?" Not waiting for a response he added, "But Copernicus did not publish his findings until after his death. Stan, you have to admit that was hardly courageous." The broad grin returned, Powell was pleased with himself.

Stanley paused, looking up at the statue of the seated young Copernicus gazing up into the sky - compass in one hand, and a heavenly sphere in the other. Stanley paused in respect to the accomplishment of this great Pole. The courage he had to have to do what was right, even when it wasn't accepted by the society of the day.

After reflecting, Stanley began, "This statue was unveiled in 1830 here at this site. It was damaged by the Germans after the insurrection in '44. They removed it from this site and intended to melt it down. Before they could take it to melt it down, they were driven off."

Stanley continued. "The remnants of the statue were found in a railcar, prepared for shipment to be destroyed. The Poles recovered the damaged statue, repaired it and returned it to this site. Here it remains in front of the reconstructed neo-classical *Staszic Palace*, which today houses the Polish Academy of Sciences."

Stanley watched Powell carefully. Having peppered him with facts, he would now make his most impactful point.

Stanley added, "Copernicus was an absolute genius, and while he did have to be leery of the wrath of the Church, he actually published his life works, 'De Revolutionibus Orbium Coelestium,' Latin for 'On the Revolutions of the Heavenly Spheres,' while alive in 1543. He was presented one of the first issues of his book on his deathbed."

Stanley again watched Powell's face. It did not give any ground.

Stanley continued, "I am sure your research also indicated this publication began what in science is referred to as The Copernican

Revolution, and was a major event in the evolution of science since the Renaissance. Galileo later thought enough of Copernicus's work to go to Rome and attempt not to have the Church ban his publication."

"So Stanley," retorted Powell, "you just made my point. Heliocentrism, what you call Copernicism, was really attributed to Galileo, an Italian, not Copernicus, the Pole. Your country clings to every little contribution to world culture, as if it were a major contributor along with the English, Spanish, Dutch, and Italians. Face it, Stanley, Poland is in reality, one of the world's least productive and most overrun countries in history."

Powell had decided it was time to throw the haymakers. Stanley sensed this assault was building to get his emotions raised before he switched subjects, to the work Stanley had done for the firm investigating Powell. The main discussion he needed to have with Stanley could not wait much longer.

Stanley breathed deeply and would not allow Langston the joy of drawing his emotions into the fray. "The Poles do not wish to take credit for changing the world, or to be recognized as a major culture in the world, Mr. Powell. They merely want their culture to exist. This comes from centuries of other cultures wishing to dominate them, and in some cases eliminating them altogether."

Stanley looked deeply into Powell's eyes. He saw nothing. Nothing but resentment. Resentment that he could not win?

They walked along the *Krakowskie Przedmieście*, as the Avenue opened wider and became more of a true promenade. The churches, ministries and palaces aligning the road became increasingly more monumental and beautiful. Along the way, displays of paintings from the 18th century artist Bernardo Bellotto showed the street in

1778. The results were strikingly similar.

"Stanley," Powell was now grinning as they walked, thinking he was beginning to strike a nerve in his interpreter. "I am merely arguing a point. It is what I am trained to do. Don't be offended. I can be no less argumentative than you can be cryptic. These are our professions; these are our natures."

Stanley detected the *cryptic* reference. He was now sure that Powell knew his background. He could hear Lou Cerilla warning him to "watch out, Powell only wants you so long as he needs you. And he always has to win an argument."

They walked north along the *Krakowskie Przedmieście*, past the beautiful palaces and churches until they came upon the stone column of King Sigismund III, who united the Poles under a single leader, and moved the capital from Krakow to Warsaw. He was an invader from Sweden, and Stanley waited for Langston to raise that fact. Regardless, the Poles loved him and this monument had been rebuilt many times after being brought down during wars and occupations.

"Langston, we are entering the *Stare Miasto* - Warsaw's Old Town," Stanley said.

"Or not so old town," retorted Powell. It had now been the better part of the afternoon since their walk had begun. The first hints of dusk settled upon the colorful pastel stucco hues of the five and six-story burgher style homes in *Stare Miasto*. They had been touring for several hours now.

Stanley began the Old Town tour. "It is true that this area was completely burned out and demolished by the Germans after the 1944 insurgency. My father was held captive here during that insurgency."

Powell looked surprised. "Really, Stanley, that was seventy years ago. Clearly he escaped, or you wouldn't be guiding me today. How did your father escape?"

Stanley thought to himself, carefully selecting his words. "There was a group of Polish citizens, held by the Germans, who were rescued by the Polish insurgents as they were pushed back and surrounded in the *Stare Miasto*. They later escaped through the sewers."

Powell decided to launch an offensive, "How interesting. Yet, it must be infuriating that the Russians never came over to assist them. But they did what I would have done, let the Poles and Germans battle it out until they wore each other out and then move in."

Powell intently watched Stanley's only reaction, which was to cock his head and swept back his long gray locks with the back of his open left palm. Stanley then steeled himself and took a few seconds to absorb the majesty of the resurrected *Stare Miasto*.

"Blessed are the hearts and hands that toiled in this effort", the old spy thought, "for they prove that no one can rip from the soul that which it holds dear."

Then thinking of his parents, "Just as no one can push from their soul the terrors it was once forced to bear."

"My father was chained to a pipe in a courtyard like a dog. Chained to his waist was a young Polish maiden. Their captivity was the work of a demented German SS officer named Keller."

Langston's eyebrows arched in amazement.

"Stanley, I am really sorry to hear that. How horrible for them. And for you to have to have to carry that with you." Langston sounded sincere, until he added "How horrible that your father didn't keep all this from you."

"Just the contrary," Stanley reacted. "How horrible if he had." He looked at Powell, whose face was now showing some of the strain of the lengthy tour.

Stanley had registered the disrespect for his father, but said nothing. He noted that Powell had been instinctively following his lead through the old town. He was pleased to see that in these unfamiliar surroundings, Langston was yielding this small bit of control. It would be a small but pivotal capitulation leading to his downfall.

Stanley continued as they walked through the narrow streets of Warsaw's Old Town. The onset of night was deepening in the narrow thoroughfares as he began to tell the end of the tale to Powell.

"They were chained together for days, with no water or food, only so that Keller could continue to return and rape that young woman."

"Your father did nothing?" Powell asked accusingly.

"Yes, yes, he did. Despite having been in Auschwitz for over three years, and being near death himself, he did something very dramatic. But I will tell you that when we reach that site."

They walked through the maze of narrow streets lined with pastel buildings, looking more a mix of Italian and Scandinavian than Powell would have guessed.

"It's beautiful, Stanley," conceded Powell. "I have to admit that the rebuilders of this area did a fantastic job."

They had stopped in a narrow alley in front of a yellow, pretty building bearing a plaque in Polish to a Marie Sklowdowska.

"This, Langston, I have saved towards the end of our walk. This is the birthplace and childhood home of Marie Sklowdowska, you might know her by her more common married name, Madame Curie."

Stanley pressed on. "She was the first woman to win the Nobel Prize, and the only woman to win it twice. She discovered the two elements, Radium and Polonium, and named the latter for her home country. She was also the first woman teacher in Paris's renowned Sorbonne University. And her daughter also won the Nobel Prize in her own right. Madame Curie - one of Poland and the world's greatest scientific minds."

"Interesting that you left out that she coined the term, *radioactive*." Langston added, as if he knew more about Madame Curie's accomplishments. "Again, this is a case where her productivity flourished only after she left Poland. France was very much an environment where she could develop under her husband, whose name she is recognized with after she won the first Nobel Prize with him."

Langston paused, and for the first time felt himself somewhat tired from the several hours of continuous walking. He went on, "She later flourished, even after his death in France. So, one could argue it was the environment, not the God-given intellect, that made her so successful."

"You can also make the same argument for all the great minds of Poland." Stanley was tensing up, tiring of Powell's constant counter arguments, intentionally demeaning Stanley's cultural pride at every turn. Stanley told himself to stay calm, and then it finally came, unexpectedly.

"Stanley, why do you not respect me?" Langston asked plaintively.

Stanley was caught off-guard by the question. He recognized Powell had now turned to the direct approach, after indirectly insulting Stanley throughout the afternoon.

Stanley responded, after a brief pause during which his eyes never left Langston's. "I do respect your business skills." Stanley felt Powell's tension coil within him.

"Stanley, that is a very evasive response. You must know by now that yesterday the Board of Directors selected me to succeed Everett Roberts. Yet all through our day together you never referenced it once. You never congratulated me a single time, Stanley. Now some men would interpret that as disrespect."

"Yes, I was aware. But I do not mean to disrespect you, Langston. I merely chose not to celebrate your selection." Stanley responded matter-of-factly.

"I never took you for a sore loser, Stanley. Clearly, I have won. I know why you were sent. I saw it coming from the beginning. That's when I began my research."

Stanley led, listening intently as they walked the narrow streets, rebuilt to match the medieval history of the old town, that opened to a large square, in the midst of which sprang a beautiful water fountain of a mermaid bearing a shield and sword. This was *Syrenka*, the cultural symbolic protector of Warsaw. This was the *Stare Miasto Rynek*, or Old Town Square.

Theirs was but one of perhaps a dozen streets, more like alleys really, emptying into this expansive rectangle of space lined with five and six story high pastel colored town homes. The houses looked like villages from a fairy tale, and the square below it buzzed with shops, artists and performers. Powell paused and took it all in, speechless for the first time Stanley had known him.

They had just entered the broad Old Town market square, lined with cafes and street vendors. A section of the square was reserved for artists offering their renditions and interpretations of Warsaw street scenes. Stanley walked into the maze of canvases, and began admiring the art. Strings of festive electric lights were buzzing alive as the square transitioned to evening.

"This is the *Rynek*, the Town Square," he stated coldly to Powell.

Langston would not allow his escape from the topic he had begun. Powell walked directly up to Stanley. Standing very close, Langston pressed his argument. "I was very surprised that you opted to join me on this trip, Stanley. I know why you were sent, and I merely wanted to get you away from the firm for a few days. The board did not need any distractions."

Stanley lifted his eyes to the hawkers of the art. He looked for Jean Paul's features among them, and found strength when he recognized him.

"Well, Langston, now that we are in the confessional, I will tell you straightaway that I filed my report before we left, clearing you of involvement in Ted Barber's death." Powell appeared surprised that Stanley had cleared him. To Stanley, his surprise could only mean by definition that his report had not leaked.

The fact that the report had been kept confidential, meant Marlow was not Powell's man.

"I knew that was your task," he said aloud, which was more confirmation that he had not seen the final report. "Why on earth would they think I had anything to do with that? It was just a coincidence that I had dinner with an associate before he got stoked up on drugs and prostitutes and ended up tumbling into a canal. Damn shame about Barber, but not my doing."

"You would never have intended to kill him, I am sure," Stanley stated, in the calm and factual manner of a debriefing from a CIA handler. The statement froze Powell instantly. "By the way, I am sure the prostitute is still not information that is generally known beyond the police themselves."

"Oh, come on, Stanley. We all know what Ted Barber was up to over there. We are not blind. We do all have our own measures of intelligence," Powell stated agitatedly.

"I am sure you were trying to discredit him even further, to reinforce the corporate reputation that you helped craft for him. Sure, he was no boy scout, but you knew Barber was allergic to cocaine. So if the man has an allergic reaction in his hotel room, only to have the answering police and medics uncover a coworker tryst with a French hooker thrown in just to make things interesting, then it discredits him before he can discredit you. I am sure you had the back end all prepared, with a team ready to snap pictures of the debauchery. They would come in handy in keeping Barber shut up."

Powell seemed to be feigning shock at this scenario.

Stanley finished, "It should have happened that way. You must have been unnerved when you heard the news that both Barber and Cecily had died that night. I guess someone had a little too heavy a hand in lacing the strawberries. Your plan goes awry, but in your own favor. Barber is now both in ill favor and permanently silent. And you feared what, that the firm would step aside from you as COO, and then CEO, because of your possible role in this tragedy?"

Langston's face clearly reacted to the last statement, and Stanley watched as he wrestled with it to gain his composure.

"You have a very active imagination, Stanley. You are wrong to even insinuate I had any knowledge or complicity in these deaths, but clearly this is not the story you fed back, or I would not have been put up for selection to the Board. What did you report back?" he asked openly.

Stanley's response was interrupted by the advance of a man selling his canvases. He spoke to Stanley in Polish for an extended period. Stanley had excused himself from Powell to purchase a rather modern interpretation of the Warsaw's Palace on the Water, where their walk had started hours before.

The man rolled the canvas into a broad roll and placed it into a cloth bag. Langston watched as Stanley passed him what appeared to be a credit card, before receiving a receipt. Powell listened as he heard the man thank Stanley, as he had learned the word "*dziękuję.*"

Stanley and Powell left the open square and now walked slowly through the maze of Old Town streets. They soon came to a large Medieval Gate, the Barbicon. Powell did not mention that it also had been rebuilt after the war, as he was on to larger sport.

"Stanley, so I find it hard to believe you sent in a report that cleared me. I am glad your research came up with the correct recommendation." Powell restarted the conversation.

"As I said, Langston," Stanley continued his debrief, looking straight ahead into the maze of narrow alleys that they now walked through, "I believed personally you were directly to blame for Barber's death, but you didn't intend to kill him. Surely a report to this end would have kept you from being named the CEO in waiting. So I reported back that you were cleared, with no mention of your laced strawberries."

He turned and read Powell's face, finding him grinding his teeth once more. Stanley went on, "Ted Barber had earlier alleged you had fixed the Daedalus Destroyer's previous error under improper funds. These errors led to innocent lives in a third world country being taken unnecessarily. Even today this would be extremely embarrassing to the firm. You couldn't have Ted popping off while you were under consideration to be the next CEO, could you? So you just needed to discredit him a little further."

"Ted and Cecily's deaths were an accident, just a little too much cocaine in the top of a couple of strawberries, accidentally taking Cecily's life, and driving Barber into a rage."

Stanley drove the last segment directly into Powell, looking straight into his lifeless eyes. "Barber stumbles outside in a drug allergy-induced state, and falls into the canal. Not all part of the original plan, was it? It wouldn't be fair to bring that up in my report, would it?"

He could see in the fine crevices of Powell's hardened face that he had hit home. Powell was only now realizing how good Stanley was at what he did.

"Your imagination is legendary, Stanley." Powell was peering at him, staring directly into his eyes, focusing somewhere on the inside of his skull. Stanley could see his jaw grinding hard now, his teeth clenched. The jaw unclenched and he unleashed the heavy artillery.

"Yes, Stanley, I did my homework. I know you're ex-CIA. I know all about your background under Marc Constantine. There was the Bryce Weldon affair back in the eighties, when you first worked with the firm. That didn't work out so well for you, did it? You helped catch this young traitor, only to have him commit suicide while in the custody of the agency."

Powell was staring hard into Stanley's eyes. Stanley steadied himself for Powell's final assault.

"Then the CIA sent you to run the Polish and Lithuanian network, deep behind the Iron Curtain. In the early nineties, the Iron Curtain falls with an unanticipated thud, and you are left with an intelligence ring nobody needs anymore and nearly $5 million in CIA funds unaccounted for. How active was your imagination then?"

Stanley calmed his face to show no response. Langston's data was dead accurate. He clearly was getting information from within the agency, and confirming exactly what Stanley had suspected.

"So, Stanley, they bring you back stateside, and although you hung on for another several years, you eventually get drummed out of the CIA. Nobody can find the $5 million, but that is chump change to them, so they throw you out and forget about you. With a retirement pension, mind you – that is something you would never have gotten from me, my friend. Yet you live a very nice comfortable life. Nothing showy, but very comfortable. When along comes an opportunity for you to make a second windfall investigating me. Stanley, I can only hope you were stealthier with the Poles and Russians than you were with me. You might as well have had a cowbell around your damn neck."

They had walked away from the Old Town along a more

modern boulevard until coming to Krasiński Square. There stood the Monument to the Warsaw Uprising, commemorating the Insurrection of August, 1944. A massive granite and bronze memorial depicted the Polish Home Army, and its house-to-house, rubble-to-rubble fighting against the German Wehrmacht. It was built in several oversized bronze elements – a long metallic rendition of a crumbling brick wall, with separate clusters of metallic insurgents emerging out of the rubble.. Even in the foreground, a few larger-than-life bronze insurgents clammored into the sewers to make their escape. The separate elements gave it a haunting three-dimensional perspective. Stanley had been here many times, and had long ago picked this site for the end of the Warsaw walking tour.

Powell persisted, not having evoked the response from Stanley that he had wanted. "So, Stanley, why so suddenly quiet? We stand here today in one of your favorite places. You have made yet more dishonest money for yourself, and I have been named the next CEO of one of the world's largest defense firms. So, Stanley, we both have won in a way."

Powell went on to press his superiority. "Stanley, your money is nothing. You'll rot off of it until you die. I will go on to lead this company to new heights, and make the world a much safer place in the same time. Stanley, clearly, I am the winner here. Your days working in any capacity for the firm are over, my friend."

Stanley stood motionless before Langston. He held his bag and its rolled-up artwork from the old town square in front of him like an over-sized fig leaf to hide his nakedness.

He looked at the heroic bronze figures of the Polish Insurgent Army emerging from the rubble to fight the Nazis. This was the very site of the pivotal battle they lost. However, not all battles lost mean defeat, often these are turning points in history that the vanquished use to propel them on to even greater victories.

"Mr. Powell," he started slowly, "in this square the Nazis fought back fiercely against the Polish Underground. The insurgents, what was left of them, escaped into the Old Town from which we just traveled. But before that, many escaped through the sewers, as is depicted here. The Nazis trapped the remainder of them in Old Town and killed them, as they liked to say, like wild dogs. You would say that the Nazis won."

Stanley had led Powell around the outer element of the sculpture, so they were now obscured between two masses of bronze. He continued, satisfied they were positioned where he wanted them.

"The Nazis then punished the Poles by systematically destroying the Old Town, the presidential palace, and most of Warsaw in yet another attempt to wipe the Polish people from the face of their very land. But here we are. Nearly seventy years later, the city is faithfully reconstructed, and is now one of the most prosperous cities in Eastern Europe. The Poles have their country, have their language, have their culture. So I would say, the Poles won."

"Stanley," Powell said with a pained expression. "Nobody cares." He paused. "Your history, your literature, your culture. Nobody cares. Today is different. It's about money, it's about power, it's about control, Stanley." Again, he paused. "I have the control, I have won."

"Was it not about money and power and control to the Nazis in the 1930s and 1940s?" Stanley could hear his father ask in his head.

Stanley had walked away from Powell as they talked. Powell instinctively followed, pressing his points. They had walked around the monument until they were obstructed from the darkening street by the monument itself.

"I care," Stanley said to Powell. "I care enough to show you a memento from the fighting in this square in the very midst of the uprising."

He stood face to face with Langston. Stanley slowly pushed his fist down into the center of the rolled-up Warsaw canvas. From within its very center, he drew an object, sleek and metallic. Langston watched as Stanley drew the Luger out by its barrel, before grasping it in a firing position and leveling it in his right hand at Powell.

"Langston, it has been a long day. Let me tell you just a little more history."

He could see Powell's surprise at being trapped in the very shadows of the monument. He saw beads of sweat form instantly across his forehead as the gun was directed threateningly at his mid-section.

Powell regained his composure. His voice was tight, but he managed to say aloud. "Stanley, you are not strong enough to do this. I know this is nothing but a scare tactic. If you hurt me, then you have no future."

Stanley stared calmly into Powell's logic.

"I already have no future, Mr. Powell. Everyone I have loved has long been taken from me. No family, no loved ones, nothing to lose except my freedom and my life. I only have a past that I carry like a cancer. It consumes my days. I now only live to satisfy the three promises I made to my dying father."

Powell's shadowed face was awash in a mix of fear, confusion and hopelessness. The dark of night was falling hard on the two men in the square.

"Before my parents died they told me the story that took place in this very area. But first my father made me make three promises - first, to always remember my Polish heritage; second, to take care of my mother after he died; and finally to never allow the strong to take advantage of the weak."

Now Stanley looked into Powell's eyes and saw terror. He did not know if it was the thought of the weapon pointed at him, or that for once in a very long time he recognized that he was not in control?

"Langston, my father, as I have said, was chained like a dog to a pipe in this area. Handcuffed to his waist was a poor peasant girl who a German named Keller kept for the sole purpose of raping, while she was secured to my father's very waist shackles. One day my father was able to get a sharp shard of brick from a mortar that exploded into the building above his head. When he was not consoling the poor, peasant girl, he was carving at the leather straps that bound his bleeding skeletal wrists. My father had survived over three years in Auschwitz, and had been barely kept alive for his language skills. Keller kept him in case he needed to escape the Russians, who as you so insensitively put it, were sitting across the river and waiting for the Poles and Germans to knock each other into oblivion."

Powell's eyes were seized on the Luger. How old was it? Did it even fire?

"My father cared for the girl. But the girl, as shocked as she was by the German brutality, consoled my father. She had never seen any-one who was so close to death, a skeleton draped with the tortured remnants of what was once a young man. They both were chained together in the courtyard; each knew that Keller would return for his pleasures. That is, their terrors."

"He came at deep dusk, much like this hour. He was angry. He was scared at the fury of the Poles, and the pending arrival of the Red Army, but would not show it. My father wore his now freed leather strand wrapped loosely about his wrist, but Keller did not notice. His only greeting to them both was in German, 'Good. You are both still alive.'

Stanley could see Powell's mind racing. He was thinking now, trying to develop a course of action. Should he just shout for help, dash from behind the monument?

Powell was sure Stanley had just left his prints all over the Luger. Did this retired spy have any conscious realization of what he was doing?

Stanley noticed Powell watching his hands and the gun. He continued.

"He made them rise. Keller made them rise, and pushed the girl over at the waist, clawing at her dress to rape her. As before, he loosened his belt and dropped his trousers. My father could feel her tense as Keller drove himself into her. This was a ritual he had been forced to watch and feel as before. He had spent over three years watching and feeling the terror of death before him, until he could feel no more. But this was different, for with every thrust, my father could see the agony on the girl's face. She refused to cry now, but even so her face was anguished. My father knew that Keller was taking her life from her just as he had taken my father's in Auschwitz. They lived, but their lives had been taken."

Stanley paused. The gun began to waiver in his hand. Powell began to recognize Stanley's mental fragility, and now knew his fate would not rest on logic; this was an emotional crisis.

"This time he could no longer passively witness her rape, he would act." Stanley began to choke on his own words.

Langston was scanning Stanley's face now. He thought he could draw his attention away by angering him. Perhaps then Powell could attack this brittle, weak old man. After all, Powell realized he was stronger.

"Stanley," Langston spoke finally. "Is this a real story, or just a metaphor for the Nazis raping of Poland?"

Stanley raised the gun to Powell's lower chest. It still wavered with Stanley's right hand.

"This is quite real, I assure you, Langston."

Stanley could see Langston's eyes widen. Powell's nerves were showing fear, but his mind kept saying there was no way for Stanley to survive this. If he pulled that trigger, Stanley was on a countdown to his own demise. This had to be some sort of ploy to draw a confession. Langston just had to hold his ground, admit nothing. Calm his nerves. But Langston also knew if Stanley had drifted into a psychotic depression, as he feared, this was all too real.

Stanley continued, "As Keller was in the act of raping the girl, my father had loosened and undone the leather strand that bound his wrist. It was a single, though thick, strand, about two feet long. Keller finished, achieving his pleasure through asserting his power. The girl dropped to her knees, in sorrow and shame. My father waited. As he had done before, out of a sign of superiority, Keller turn his back on my father as he reached to pull up his uniform's trousers. This was the second my father had waited for."

Powell had been waiting for a second to wrestle away this Luger from the old man standing before him, but decided this was not it. He decided to continue waiting. The immediate shock of the Luger had now become a reality he was readying himself to deal with.

"My father knew he would get only one chance to act, and he knew he was weak, but in that instant, with my father standing, chained at the waist to the pipe, the girl kneeling at his feet, and Keller in the act of pulling on his trousers, his back to my father, this is when my father went into action. He threw the leather strand over Keller's head and around his neck. The struggle began. My father pulled on the leather with all his might. Keller was shocked as the leather cut into the stubbled skin of his neck. He dropped his trousers, and clutched at the leather garrote around his neck."

Stanley looked into Powell's eyes, and saw that Langston was listening intently.

"My father attempted to strangle Keller, but he was too weak from years of famine and physical neglect. Keller was able to force his fingers under the leather strand at his neck. He slowly was able to pull it from his neck, and as my father became weaker, Keller overpowered him and slowly pulled the leather strap from my father's grasp. He immediately began to whip him with it as my father, still chained to the pipe, covered the girl with his arched back. My father had failed, and Keller stepped back away from my father and the girl."

Langston Powell seemed to smile wryly at this point of the story.

"Keller reached for his trousers, but not to pull them up, but to pull his Luger, this very Luger I have trained on you at this moment, from his holster. He was shocked to find it missing. He frantically looked for it on the ground, only to spot it in the girl's hand. She had pulled it from its holster while my father struggled with Keller."

"Her name was Manya. This is the affectionate Polish name for Marie. She was the woman who would become my mother."

Before Langston could react, Stanley continued.

"Manya passed the gun to my father. Keller stood exposed before them both."

"Keller's face attempted to hide the concern for his situation. As your face attempts to do now. My father, catching his breath, leveled the gun at Keller."

Powell thought now was the very time to speak to Stanley to distract him. "So, your mother and father were trapped in a courtyard near here. Your father escapes from this and takes your mother to America, and then has a child with the very woman he watched repeatably get raped in front of him? That was their basis for bringing you into the world, Stanley?"

Stanley breathed in slowly. A flush of fury fought over every other emotion currently in him. It seemed to emanate from deep within him, but settled in the tactile nerves running through his aged wrinkled skin. He thought of the message his mother had given him ten years after his father died. The message that he received shortly before witnessing Bryce Weldon's suicide.

"My father never touched my mother. Never for that purpose. This is what he was trying to tell me as he was dying. My mother, his Manya, was a saint, blessed and to be revered. He never laid a hand on her, here in Poland nor later in London, or even in their life together in America. He never took pleasure from her. He could not bear to subject her to that after what Keller had done to her. But he never lived to tell me that."

Stanley paused. Powell could now sense the torment that grew inside his interpreter turned captor. This made Stanley an increasing threat to Powell's life. Powell decided he needed to feed Stanley's torment, force him into a mistake, or a debilitating breakdown.

"My mother, some ten years after my father's death, she had to be the person to tell me that I was the product of her being raped by this SS monster. That I had to hear this from my mother, his Manya, is but another indignity she endured." Stanley's voice was now edged with the strain of his recollections and guilt.

Powell's eyes widened into a full smirk. The corners of his mouth turned up. "Stanley, are you telling me that after all this tour of Polish heritage crap, that you are not even Polish. You are German! You are Keller's son!"

Powell had broken into a loud extended chuckle.

Stanley said, "This is why I honored the man who raised me, by remembering I am Polish, from the mother I took care of for the rest of her life." Powell's chuckle turned into a loud laugh.

Stanley continued flatly, "Keller had also begun to laugh nervously, until he saw my father switch off the gun's safety. Then his eyes narrowed." Saying this, Stanley used his right thumb to switch off the Luger's safety.

Powell's face froze in the darkened shadows that crept across the massive bronze monument.

"Stanley, let's be rational here. Why do you want to harm me? I am not a monster."

Stanley steeled his nerves. This was the moment he had lived to achieve. He had lived to defend his mother, from who's very defiling he himself was created.

He lived to honor his Polish Heritage. Damn that his biological father was a German Nazi sadist. But even this was representative of the oppression of Poland itself over the centuries. Nothing was more Polish, unfortunately.

He lived to defend the weak from the strong. He was in a position to strike hard at not just a man, but the total hierarchy of oppression in the modern era.

"'Beware those who wrestle with monsters'…said my father as he raised the Luger to Keller's chest." Stanley raised the Luger to Powell's chest. "Pulling the trigger, he said, 'I have become a monster.' Keller was shot through the heart, just another dead Nazi in the Polish rebellion."

But Stanley did not shoot Powell as he said this.

Powell waited an eternity. He convinced himself Stanley did not have the conviction to pull the trigger. Powell could see single tears running down Stanley's face. He realized that Stanley was emotionally exhausted. This exhaustion would consume Stanley, and could allow Powell to escape this incendiary moment.

Stanley had planned this out in great detail, walking Powell exhaustively, having gotten Powell to this isolated location at this hour.

Where did he get the gun? Powell had all of Stanley's bags inspected before they went on the plane; there was no gun. It was passed to him in the square along with the canvas. This had all been meticulously planned out. That fact alone struck fear in Powell's very being. But Powell sensed that the strain of the planning, the theatrics, the very dialogue they were having were taking their toll on the aged spy. Powell decided to increase that strain on him.

"Stanley," Powell began soberly, staring into his captor's eyes. "Stanley, you can't do this. There is no way you gain anything from this. You think I will confess to crimes of your imagination? I will not. You can kill me if you think there is a purpose in it, but there is none. Besides, I believe you are too weak to do this."

The shadows darkened across their faces. Powell was ready to make his lunge. Powell decided he could wrestle the gun from the old man. He just needed to get the initial jump.

"I am *weak*?" asked Stanley aloud. He looked down at the Luger and paused. He could feel a shudder, a revulsion, building within him. It swelled until it took all Stanley's power to steady himself against the waves of anger raging within him.

Then his revulsion overpowered Stanley.

"The strong always prosper at the expense of the weak," he said aloud as razors ripped through his nerves, as his muscles pulsed and twitched in agony.

At that critical point, an old Polish gentleman walked with his dog innocently around the corner of the monument. Shocked to see the gun between the two men, he excitedly uttered the Polish word *"Przepraszam"* (a startled *"excuse me"*) and in his shock stumbled back away from the monument. Stanley's head turned instinctively toward this intrusion.

Seeing Stanley distracted, Powell decided to lunge. He coiled and began to lean forward to strike.

Stanley immediately noticed the initiation of movement from Langston Powell. His years of training overtook the physical rebellion within him. Whatever it was that precluded his acting, was now washed away in almost involuntary reaction.

Stanley pushed the Luger into Powell's oncoming chest and shot a single bullet into his heart. The look of incredibility washed over Powell's face before the flash of the muzzle did. As Powell fell back and away from him, Stanley could only wonder if this was the same look that washed Keller's face in the instant of his death. Powell was certainly dead, but this did not stop Stanley from leaning over him and firing a second shot into his skull.

Stanley felt compelled to speak aloud, over the body of Langston Powell, the words of Nietzsche in German: *"Beware he who wrestles with monsters, lest he become a monster himself."*

Having fulfilled the third promise, Stanley dropped the Luger next to Langston Powell's lifeless body, turned and walked off briskly into the abyss. Soon the abyss, having stared into him for so many years, would hunt and consume him.